THE PINK CHRISTMAS COOKIE CAPER

A Paranormal Cozy Mystery

VELLA DAY

Erotic Reads Publishing

The Pink Christmas Cookie Caper

A Witch's Cove Mystery
Book 17
Copyright © 2021 Vella Day

www.velladay.com

velladayauthor@gmail.com

Cover Art by Jaycee DeLorenzo

Edited by Rebecca Cartee

Published in the United States of America

E-book ISBN: 978-1-951430-42-9

Print book ISBN: 978-1-951430-43-6

ALL RIGHTS RESERVED. No part of this book may be used or reproduced in any manner whatsoever without written permission of the author except in the case of brief questions embodied in critical articles or reviews.

This is a work of fiction. Names, characters, places, and incidents either are the product of the author's imagination or are used fictitiously, and any resemblance to actual persons living or dead, business establishments, events or locales, is entirely coincidental.

Created with Vellum

BLURB

A wacky parrot, a poisoned pink dessert, and a roomful of suspects. Merry Christmas to me!

I finally get to meet my fiancé's parents, and what happens? At the welcome party, a neighbor is murdered right under our noses. Since Jaxson and I run the Pink Iguana Sleuth Agency, we shouldn't be too shocked. We deal with dead people quite a lot.

Sheriff June Waters is not amused when we try to help solve the crime, but hey, we aren't going to stand by and do nothing. But boy, do I miss my gossip queens and the cooperation of our sheriff. However, we would adapt.

What we thought was a routine murder, turns out to be one driven by a long held secret that the killer will do anything to keep.

I usually suggest you stop by our Witch's Cove office so I can give you an update, but we won't be there. Hope Santa brought you lots of presents.

CHAPTER ONE

"I'm nervous," I told my fiancé, Jaxson Harrison, as he turned into his parents' subdivision in Magnolia, Florida. Their home was a two-hour drive from where we lived in Witch's Cove.

"Why?"

"I haven't seen your parents in what? Ten years? Back then, I was Drake's best friend."

"And now you're my fiancée, but you're still Drake's friend."

"I know."

"Glinda, this isn't like you. You know there's nothing to worry about."

"I hope so, but it will be my first Christmas not spending it with my parents. It's going to feel a bit, I don't know, strange."

He glanced over at me. "Your folks have Rihanna

and your Aunt Fern to keep them company on Christmas day. We'll be back in two days. We can celebrate Christmas with them then."

"I know. And Rihanna's mom is going to be there, too, so they will have plenty of family love on Christmas morning."

I was being selfish wanting to be with my folks, as well as with Jaxson, on that special day, but celebrating the evening of the twenty-sixth would be good enough. Last year, he and his brother, Drake, had spent the holidays with their parents, and I missed both of them. This year, we decided to split our time between the two families so that we could be together.

By the way, I'm Glinda Goodall, a not very powerful witch, who runs the Pink Iguana Sleuths Company with Jaxson. Quite often, some type of magic is involved in a crime, and when that happens, the sheriff calls on us to help solve the mystery. Thankfully, this month, nothing has been stolen nor has anyone been murdered, which meant we were free to travel.

Jaxson ran a quick hand over my arm. "You know, it will be nice to relax and not have to hunt down a murderer or try to find some stolen object for a change. Think about it. If we're here, we won't be tempted to find trouble."

"That's true." The problem was that I kind of liked having something to do. I wasn't an idle hands type of person.

Jaxson pulled into the driveway and parked. "I see Drake and Andorra beat us here." He pulled in next to their vehicle.

I was excited to spend time with my two good friends. I'd only reunited with Andorra, a high school acquaintance, a few months ago, but we'd bonded quickly, partly because we worked together to solve a murder—a pretty commonplace occurrence for me. As for Drake, we'd been inseparable since middle school. But then I met Jaxson, and shall we say, the rest is history.

The outside of the Harrison's brick home was decorated with Christmas lights—a lot of Christmas lights—and lawn ornaments, which included a Santa and sleigh on top of the roof. A second set of illuminated reindeers littered the lawn, as did some playful elves. I couldn't wait until it was dark. The visual effect would be stunning.

Jaxson cut the engine. "Remember, my mom's name is Maddy and my dad—"

"Yes, is Eugene. I remember." We'd been over this a few times. Maybe that was because back in high school, they were just Mr. and Mrs. Harrison.

Iggy, my familiar, who had ridden over on my lap, lifted his head. "I bet Mrs. Harrison won't recognize me."

"Why is that? It isn't as if there were a lot of pink iguanas." At least in Florida there weren't.

"I'm so big now."

"That's true." I turned to Jaxson. "I hadn't thought of it, but I wonder if Drake and Andorra will want your folks to meet Hugo." That was Andorra's familiar, though it would be harder to explain what looked like a grown man to her boyfriend's parents.

"Hugo might come?" Iggy asked.

The hope in his voice tore at my soul. Hugo was Iggy's best friend. Andorra never mentioned that Hugo might be there, but perhaps she could call the Hex and Bones Apothecary, the town's occult store that her grandmother owned, and ask him to stop by. After all, the gargoyle shifter could teleport. "We'll see, but no promises."

"Okay," he said, not sounding all that optimistic.

I twisted toward Jaxson. "Did Drake say anything about why he invited Andorra? I mean, asking a girlfriend for Christmas implies something might happen." As in, was he going to ask her to marry him?

Jaxson chuckled. "I have no idea, and even if I did, I wouldn't tell you." He tapped my nose and then pushed open the door.

"Fine, don't tell me." I placed Iggy in my purse and then eased out of the truck. The back seat held presents and our suitcases. "Should we take all of this inside now?"

"Let's leave everything for now."

My nerves shot up, which was irrational. I'd only

gained about twenty pounds since high school, but I was a bit self-conscious about it.

Jaxson knocked and then opened the door. "Hello?"

"Is that you, Jaxson?" a female voice called.

Was his mother expecting someone else? As if a beehive had been poked, Drake, Andorra, and an older couple emerged from another room—the den or the kitchen perhaps? I couldn't guess which room was in the back, because the inside of the house looked like a Christmas showroom. Santas, elves, stockings hung with care over the fireplace, giant candy canes, and three-feet tall toy soldiers filled every nook and cranny. And here, I thought my mom was a fanatic because of her love of the movie, *The Wizard of Oz*, but she paled in comparison to Jaxson's mother.

"Hi, Mom." Jaxson hugged her.

She leaned back and ran her gaze up and down his body. "You look...wonderful. And happy." Maddy Harrison turned to me. "Oh, Glinda, it's wonderful to see you again. Thank you for giving my son his glow." She grinned.

Before I could respond to that compliment, I found myself in a super human bear hug. "You, too, Mrs. H."

"She's squishing me!" That plea came from Iggy.

As graciously as I could, I leaned back. "Iggy's in my bag."

"Oh, I am so sorry. Can I see him?"

I was pleased she remembered that Iggy was a male. "Sure."

I lifted him out, and she squealed. "He's as cute as I remember. May I hold him?"

People usually didn't make that request. "Iggy? What do you say?"

"Tell her not to hold me too tight."

I handed him to her. "Be gentle."

Maddy immediately dragged her hand lightly over his dorsal crest. I waited for him to complain, but he seemed to like it. Maybe we'd get through this vacation without drama after all.

His dad patted Jaxson on the back and then faced me. "Glinda Goodall. Aren't you a sight for sore eyes."

I held out my hand, but he hugged me instead. "Nice to see you again too."

His skin was a bit more sallow than I remember, but that could be because he'd been ill a few months ago.

As for Jaxson's mom, she was still a beauty—tall, fit, with shoulder length salt and pepper hair, and a perfect smile that lit up the room.

"Where are my manners? You guys must be tired. Come sit down. Can I get you anything to drink?"

If she hadn't sounded like she wanted to fix us something, I would have said no. "Some coffee would be great."

"Perfect. And for you, darling?"

"The same, but Glinda likes it with cream and sugar."

"No problem. I'll be right back." She handed Iggy back to me. I would have asked if he was okay, but he seemed to have lasered his focus on the parrot in the cage.

I hoped that wouldn't be a problem. Iggy had issues with birds.

"They have a parrot!" Iggy said in a tone that sounded more like a growl.

I remember when they took in Pete. "I forgot about him," I whispered, "but he's not a seagull. And he's in a cage, so you don't have worry." Iggy had an ongoing war with a local seagull he'd named Tippy. "Tippy is white and this bird is red with blue wings. They don't look anything alike."

"Maybe, but I'm not taking any chances," he said.

I had no idea what he meant by that. I hoped he wouldn't be a problem for Iggy. Right now, I wanted to concentrate on Jaxson's folks.

I walked over to the seating area in the living room, where my friends had parked themselves, probably so that I could spend a moment with the loving Harrisons.

"Hey, guys," I said.

Andorra and Drake stood and gave me a hug. "Good ride over?" Drake asked.

I smiled. "Uneventfully good."

Eugene joined us and motioned we take the sofa,

while he, Andorra, and Drake sat in large comfy chairs that were more or less in front of the fully decorated Christmas tree. Underneath, presents were piled high. Oh, my.

His dad leaned forward. "Glinda, in case you forgot, Maddy still goes overboard on everything." He swung his arm around the room. "Later this afternoon, we are having a neighborhood Christmas party, so be prepared for more overload."

I doubted it would be more over-the-top than her decorated home. "I'm sure it will be fun to meet all of your neighbors."

Jaxson's mom returned with our drinks. She set the tray down on the large wooden coffee table and then took the chair next to her husband. "I heard Eugene warn you about our small get together. It's just some neighbors and a few of the City Council members that the boy's dad works with."

I thought their father was retired. Jaxson needed to do a better job of updating me.

"So, Glinda, how are your folks, and what have you been doing since high school?" Maddy asked. "I only know what Drake and Jaxson tell me. And you know boys. They don't say much."

"I know what you mean." I told them about what my parents had been up to and then about my one year teaching stint to middle school math students. That not so great experience prompted me to change my profession to waitressing at my aunt's restaurant. "As you can see, just your usual upbringing." I smiled.

I didn't need to remind them that after that, Jaxson had been accused of murder, and I had helped prove he had been framed. That resulted in us joining forces to open our Pink Iguana Sleuths company.

"I will be eternally grateful for you believing in Jaxson and helping him prove he was framed."

"I'm the lucky one," I said as I squeezed Jaxson's hand.

Okay, we were getting a little sappy here, but it was nice to see how much the Harrisons adored their sons. We spent the next hour talking about Drake's plans for his cheese and wine shop, and then Maddy asked whether Andorra planned to take over the occult store when her grandmother retired.

"Probably. Elizabeth and I make a good team."

When there was no mention of Hugo, I sensed no one had told the Harrisons about him or his gargoyle-shifting girlfriend.

Maddy stood. "The guests will be arriving in an hour. I bet you four would like to freshen up. Andorra, can you show Glinda to your room?"

"Sure."

"Jaxson," Maddy said. "You'll bunk with Drake in his room."

"Great." Jaxson turned to me. "I'll get the luggage and deliver it to your room."

Between the suitcases and the presents, he'd need help. "I can carry a few things."

Drake held up a hand. "We got this. You two get ready."

That was code for him wanting to chat with Jaxson about something—alone.

"Come on, Glinda," Andorra said.

With Iggy in hand, I followed her into a room that was definitely all male. It had a twin bed covered with a plaid bedspread. Next to it was a cot. I stepped over to the desk. "She kept Jaxson's wrestling trophies from high school?"

I couldn't recall when his parents had moved from Witch's Cove to Magnolia, but I believe it was after Jaxson had been arrested for a theft he was later cleared of.

"She's nostalgic. It's sweet and creepy at the same time. It's the same with Drake's room. He tried to toss some of his stuff when he came home the last time, but his mom said it kept her sons close to have their memorabilia in the house."

"I always thought it odd that Derek even has a room here since he remained in Witch's Cove after they moved," I said. Jaxson did live here for a while, so he would have a room.

"I know, but when they moved, Maddy said it was easier to just duplicate the house."

That was sad in a way. Iggy wiggled, and I placed

him on the cot. "Maybe you should stay in here during the party," I told him. "We don't need you to be trampled on."

"You mean attacked by that bird. It's a parrot, yet it hasn't said anything. What's up with that? Do you think he's like Hugo and can't talk?"

"I have no idea."

Jaxson came in with my suitcase. "Mom said the get together is a casual affair, but that means wear a dress."

I smiled. "Gotcha."

"Oh, and she has sandwiches in the kitchen. This Christmas affair is a dessert party, and I told her we were hungry for real food."

I grinned. He was hungry for real food. Me? I had a sweet tooth. "I'll be right out as soon as I jump in the shower."

"You go ahead," Andorra said. "I just need to change."

As I dashed into the attached bath, Iggy asked Andorra if Hugo could visit. I didn't hear her response, but it would be better if she let him down instead of me.

I quickly cleaned up. When I stepped into the bedroom with a towel wrapped around me, Andorra had changed into a lovely sapphire blue dress.

"You look really nice," I said.

She smiled. "Thanks. I'm going to head to the kitchen. I'm starving."

"I'll be right out."

In short order, I changed and joined everyone. Not only was there a plate of delicious looking sandwiches on the counter, Maddy had a large plate of brownies topped with pink frosting as well as another plate of sugar cookies with pink frosting on display.

"Is someone else a pink fan?" I hadn't seen anything else pink in the house. Red and green had dominated the Christmas theme.

Jaxson chuckled "No, this is for you. It's partially my fault. I might have mentioned a time or two that your favorite color is pink. Mom just wanted to make you feel at home, and as usual, she went a little overboard."

"I think it's sweet." I grabbed a sandwich and a bottle of water and sat on the stool at the island.

Drake moaned. "I forgot how good Magnolia Deli's roast beef sandwiches are."

He was right. The meat was cooked to perfection. For the next fifteen minutes, we chowed down and said little. The kitchen was in the rear of the house in a separate room, but the distinctive doorbell chime filtered back to us.

Jaxson tossed his napkin on his plate, picked up the dish, and stood. "Showtime!"

This was going to be fun.

CHAPTER TWO

As soon as we cleaned up our dishes, Jaxson, Drake, Andorra, and I headed into the main room. A couple who were close to sixty came in carrying a pink cake. Pink, really? I know, I know, I was the last person in the world to judge. I did love that color, but I was okay with some variety—especially at Christmas.

Maddy grinned and waved the four of us over. She introduced us to Mary Jo and Sid Harper. "Mary Jo is on the City Council with Eugene."

Sid worked at some local manufacturing plant. From what I could figure out, Jaxson's dad was a consultant to the Mayor, but I didn't probe what he did for him.

Mary Jo smiled at me. "Maddy said your favorite color was pink." She lifted the cake.

I couldn't deny it since I'd worn a dusty rose dress.

I'm afraid my fancy wardrobe was a bit lacking. But why not have something to represent Andorra, too? "It is."

Maddy pointed to the room behind the living room. "Let me put that on the table for you."

"Thanks."

I could work a crowd with the best of them. After all, I had years of practice waitressing and engaging the customers. I really shone when I needed information for a case, but this situation was very different. Standing in the hallway with two strangers was downright awkward.

Thankfully, Jaxson's dad came to the rescue. He strode up to them and shook their hands. "Why, if it isn't the Harpers. Come inside, and I'll fix you two a drink." Eugene turned to Jaxson. "Can you put their coats in your old room?"

"Sure."

I hoped Iggy didn't have a fit. He tended to be territorial and might interpret the coats as interlopers.

When Jaxson returned, two more couples had arrived. This time when Eugene introduced us, I forgot their names seconds after they told them to me.

I leaned closer to Jaxson. "How many people did your mom invite?"

"I don't know, but if last year is any indication, maybe twenty?"

That was a big party. "We need name tags."

He laughed. "Don't worry. There won't be a quiz,

and I doubt you'll see any of these people again until next year."

I found some relief in that. For the next twenty minutes, there was a steady stream of people, each of whom came with a dessert—make that a pink dessert.

Personally, I would have gone with something a bit more Christmassy, but I appreciated Maddy's attempt to make me feel included.

Jaxson placed a hand on my back. "We should head to the dining room and have some dessert. We'll meet the stragglers as they come in."

I was happy with that. When we stepped into the room, Mary Jo was chatting with a younger man, who Jaxson remembered was Armand. I'm sure his last name wasn't Hammer, though. I chuckled to myself at my bad joke.

"It's wrong to tear down the fair," Mary Jo snarled as we stepped by those two. "It's a city icon. I can't understand why you don't realize that. I took my kids there every summer when they were little. The Magnolia Fairgrounds should remain sacred."

Her voice had risen above the din. Oh, my. I looked up at Jaxson. "Do you know what that was about?" I asked as soon as we moved out of their earshot.

"Kind of. One group wants to put a strip mall in where the fairgrounds are, and the other wants to keep it the way it is."

That could be an issue. "That reminds me of the

Hightower's debate over whether to tear down our historic theatre."

"You're right. Let's hope this issue doesn't end in death like that one did." He flashed me a grin.

I shivered. Someone placed a hand on my shoulder. "Glinda, come have some dessert," Maddy said.

I turned around and smiled. "Of course. I think I'll have one of your brownies."

"Good choice." She turned to Jaxson. "Hon, can you take this tray of cookies to the living room for me?"

"Sure, Mom."

As soon as Jaxson left, I grabbed a napkin and a brownie and then took a bite. I hadn't planned on groaning, but I couldn't help it. They were delicious.

"So you're Jax's fiancée, I hear." I spun around to find a cherubic looking man with thinning brown hair and glasses.

"I am. I'm Glinda."

"I'm Wilson Eberhart. I live next door." He leaned in closer—a little too close. Can we say boundaries?

"Nice to meet you, Mr. Eberhart." I tried to sound welcoming.

He grabbed a sugar cookie with the pink frosting. "I like the pink theme."

He must have heard about my penchant for that color. "Me, too, but I also like real Christmas cookies." As in red and green ones.

Wilson pressed his lips together and slightly shook

his head. "I don't think everyone here is a *believer*, if you know what I mean. Pink is a neutral color. It's like green or yellow for a baby shower when you don't know the sex."

What an odd comment. I wondered what the non-believers thought of all the Christmas decorations then? "I get it."

"A word of advice?" he whispered.

I looked to see if Jaxson had returned from his errand, but he hadn't. This man was rather strange. "Yes?"

"If anyone asks your opinion about the fairgrounds debate, don't answer."

"Why is that?" I could guess, but I was interested to hear his take.

He shook his head. "Half the town wants to tear down the fair so they can put in a new mall that will house a walk-in clinic, two restaurants, and a few trendy shops. The other half wants to keep the status quo. Our town is all about tradition, you know."

I couldn't quite tell which side he was on, but if I had to guess, I'd say he'd vote to keep the fair.

Before Mr. Eberhart could continue, Jaxson came over. "Wilson, let's not monopolize my fiancée's time. I want Glinda to meet the others."

"Oh, of course." Keeping his gaze lowered, he backed away. "Nice to meet you, Glinda."

"You too." Jaxson led me into the living room where

many had congregated. I noted that almost everyone had a drink in one hand and some goodies in the other. "Thanks for saving me."

"I'm sorry I didn't get to you sooner. In case you couldn't tell, Wilson is the town's gossip."

"I'm not surprised. Every town seems to have one or two." In the case of Witch's Cove, we probably had eight or ten. Those were my favorite people.

"Tear it down," the parrot squawked. "Tear it down."

So he could talk. "I guess I know what he'd vote for."

Jaxson chuckled. "So it seems."

We were about to speak with another couple, when a high piercing scream erupted from the dining room. What in the world? Jaxson took off, and then Drake rushed past me, before Andorra grabbed my arm and tugged.

"Come on," she said.

"You go." Almost everyone was rushing to the dining room to see what was going on, and they couldn't even get in. I figured I might learn more out here.

"Okay." She hustled toward the dining room but had to wait with the others to see what was happening.

I realize a person had screamed, but I figured someone probably had knocked one of the desserts off the table and had made a mess. I wouldn't have thought that would have warranted such a reaction, but what did I know?

A minute later, Eugene parted the crowd and stepped into the living room, his cell phone in hand. I strode over to him. "What happened?"

"Armand Linfield collapsed. I need to call 9-1-1." Jaxson's dad made the call.

Jaxson then emerged from the dining room and pulled me aside. "I can't believe this. Armand Linfield, who is a City Councilman, is dead.

"Dead? That's not what your dad said. Maybe this man had a heart attack and is still alive. Is someone giving him CPR at least?"

"I don't know, but he's only forty."

Forty-year-olds died from heart attacks more often than people were led to believe. Intense sobs floated out from the dining room. The last place I wanted to be was in there. "I think I'll sit down and think."

A couple left the dining room and came up to Jaxson. "Where did you put our coats?"

"I'll show you."

Instantly, my sleuth hat appeared. I jumped up and rushed over to Jaxson's dad who was now off the phone. "I know you're busy, but can you get me some paper and a pen? We need to write down the names of those who leave."

"Why?" he asked.

Wasn't it obvious? "The police will want to question everyone in case someone *helped* this Armand fellow collapse. We need to tell them who left."

"You're right."

When the couple returned with their coats, Eugene went over to them. I couldn't hear what he said, but they handed their coats back to Jaxson and then sat down in the living room. Eugene must have agreed with me since he asked the rest of the guests who had wished to leave to stay for a bit.

Jaxson returned. "And here I thought this was going to be a calm holiday weekend."

"Do you think we have bad karma? Wherever we go, death seems to follows," I said.

He clasped my shoulders and faced me. "No, and we aren't positive the Councilman is dead, though it sure looks like he is."

"Right. We don't need to be jumping to conclusions so soon. It's not like he was shot or anything."

"No."

Sirens sounded in the background, and then the flashing lights shone in through the window. A knock on the door followed.

Jaxson opened it, and a rather tall woman, wearing a beige uniform that was a bit too tight around her middle came in. Her slightly graying brown hair was cut almost military short. While her long sleeves prevented me from seeing her arms, I bet she'd be formidable in a fight.

Jaxson nodded to her. "Sheriff Waters."

"Jaxson. Trouble is still following you around, I see."

Really? That was not a neighborly thing to say. From her comment, the sheriff was all too aware of his criminal record. I hope she also knew that after Jaxson's accuser confessed that he'd lied under oath, Jaxson's record had been expunged. Her comment was totally uncalled for.

Two paramedics rushed in with medical bags slung over their shoulders. I hadn't seen the body, but I had the sense it might be too late for Armand.

"I'll show you to the dining room," Jaxson said.

The sheriff followed Jaxson and the paramedics. As much as I wanted to take a peek, the room was still crowded, even though many of the guests had retreated to the living room.

Andorra slipped out and motioned I join her in the bedroom. I rushed to catch up to her. Once we were inside our bedroom, she closed the door most of the way. I figured she wanted to be able to hear if anything major happened.

"It's bad, Glinda."

"I'm guessing that man died?"

"He did."

"Did you see what happened?" I asked.

"No. When Drake and I got there, he was already on the floor, but one of the sugar cookies with the pink frosting was in his hand. I think he was poisoned."

That was a huge leap. "Maddy made those."

"I know. Maybe that's why she's kind of in shock right now."

"If I had a guest drop dead at my party, I'd be upset too. Where's Drake?"

"With his mom," Andorra said. "I have to give her credit, though. Even through her own tears, she was trying to comfort the man's wife."

Iggy crawled down from the cot. "I'll go investigate."

"You will stay right here, young man."

He spun around to face me. "Don't worry. I'll be invisible. No one will know I'm there. I'll listen real good and report back."

Before I could tell him not to leave, he cloaked himself. Because he was invisible, someone could step on him. I hope he used the walls to get around instead of the floor—assuming he could climb the slick surface.

"I wish Hugo and Genevieve were here. They could stay cloaked for a long time," Andorra said. She was aware that Iggy couldn't reliably maintain his invisibility.

I snapped my fingers. "Why not ask them to come? She and Hugo could be here in seconds. But tell them they can't just pop up out of thin air like they usually do. Everyone would freak."

"I'll contact her, but you know that every time she teleports, it's to a place she knows. She's never been here."

"Genevieve can't track your phone or something?" I asked.

She chuckled. "You think gargoyle shifters come with an internal GPS?"

"I don't know, but she was able to track down the girlfriend of one of our suspects a while back. I don't remember giving her the address."

Andorra blew out a breath. "I'll give her a call."

Yes! "Put her on speaker."

She rolled her eyes. "What I do for a friend."

Andorra called Genevieve. When she didn't pick up after seven rings, I was about to suggest to Andorra that she call her cousin who worked in the store where Hugo and Genevieve resided.

"Hello?" Genevieve sounded out of breath.

"Hey, it's Andorra. Where are you?"

"Sorry, I'm with...um...Hugo. We're up on the church where we used to reside."

Reside? She meant where they were gargoyle statues. I didn't want to think what she and Hugo were doing there. I leaned closer. "This is Glinda. We had a death or possible murder at Jaxson's parents' house and could use your help."

"We can come." She sounded excited.

I pumped a fist. I nodded to Andorra that she needed to give Genevieve directions to the house.

"When you get here, can you two remain cloaked?" I

asked. "We don't need anyone knowing you are magical beings."

"Sure."

Before disconnecting, Andorra told her where the Harrison's lived.

I wasn't sure how long it would take them to get here. "I'm going to check on Jaxson."

I hadn't reached the door when both of our gargoyle shifters appeared. No matter how many times they teleported, I was always surprised to see them materialize.

Andorra stepped over to them. "Thanks for coming."

"What do you need us to do?" Genevieve asked.

"The sheriff and her deputies are in the dining room with the body, but a lot of the guests are in the living room. Maybe you could divide and conquer?"

"Okay." Genevieve faced Hugo and telepathed something to him. He then disappeared.

"You did tell him to remain cloaked, right?" I wasn't sure why I was so paranoid, but it was possible Jaxson wouldn't want us to get involved in this murder and bring more attention to his parents.

"Of course. We're not rookies, you know." She winked.

That lightened the mood. "Thanks."

Andorra and I returned to the main part of the house. I found Jaxson in the dining room speaking with the sheriff. His mom was kneeling down next to a woman who was sobbing. Andorra said she was the victim's wife. A medical examiner and his assistant were attending to the body.

There were about five couples standing around watching and whispering. If that wasn't awkward, I don't know what was.

Once Jaxson noticed me, he said something to the sheriff and then came over to me.

"Any idea what happened?" I asked.

CHAPTER THREE

"THE MAN DIED," Jaxson said.

"Andorra told me that. Do you know if it was a heart attack?"

"We know nothing yet," he said. "It could have been a brain aneurysm, for all we know. No one is saying it's murder, but I'm betting it was."

A uniformed officer entered the dining room. "If I could have everyone's attention, please. There is a deputy in the living room. Once he takes down your name and contact information, you are free to go." The group mumbled. "Please understand, we have to process the scene."

I didn't want to be in the room anyway. As I followed the others out, I tried to catch a glimpse of the corpse. All I could see was his hand—a hand that was holding a pink sugar cookie, just like Andorra said.

While the deputy jotted down the names of those in the living room, Eugene gathered their coats and then passed them out to their owners.

Jaxson's dad must have explained to the deputy that the four of us were staying at the house since the only thing he asked us was whether we saw anything.

As the two men rolled the body out on a gurney, Maddy came out with Armand's wife. Such a tragedy. She and her husband were relatively young, and I couldn't even imagine her loss.

Jaxson's mom went up to Eugene. "I'm going to take Lydia home. She called her sister, who's going to stay with her."

Eugene kissed his wife goodbye. Once they each grabbed their coats, they left.

The sheriff then spoke with Eugene. "I'm sure you had nothing to do with Armand's death but stay in town in case we need to ask you any more questions."

Jaxson's dad opened his mouth to say something, but then he merely nodded. Smart man. Once the sheriff's department and medical examiner's team took off, we were finally alone.

Jaxson went over to his father. "Come sit down, Dad. Let me get you something to drink."

"How about some coffee?" Eugene asked.

"Sure."

I followed Jaxson into the kitchen. "What did the sheriff say?" I asked.

"You couldn't pry information out of Jane Waters even if you waterboarded her."

"She sounds tougher than Steve." At least our sheriff believed in sharing information if need be. Steve Rocker understood the power of gossip to help him solve a case. I wonder if Jane Waters was the same.

"Jane definitely is a determined woman. Even if we wanted to offer some assistance, it wouldn't be easy. She doesn't like me."

So it seemed. "Does she know you were framed for the liquor store theft?" The stigma of being incarcerated would probably never leave him.

"She does, but she's still leery of me. At least she likes Drake."

"That's good. If we need to find out anything, we'll use him as our liaison."

"That would be best." Jaxson poured the coffee for his dad, and I followed him out. He handed his father the steaming cup and then sat down next to him. I took the chair next to Andorra and leaned close. "Is Hugo here?"

She nodded and then mouthed the words, *both of them are*.

"We probably should let them get back to Witch's Cove. The guests have left, so there is nothing for them to do."

Andorra closed her eyes for a moment, I assumed it

was to telepath her request to Hugo. She inhaled and then turned to me. "They're gone."

"Who's gone?" Eugene asked.

Whoops. "The guests," I said, answering for Andorra." I hoped he believed me. "How about if Andorra and I clean up? Maddy will be terribly upset when she returns, and she doesn't need to deal with the mess."

"That would be great. I know she'd appreciate it."

Having something to do would help calm my mind. When we entered the dining room, Iggy was in the corner—visible this time. I went over and lifted him up. "Did you learn anything?"

"Yes. I learned that walls are slippery. They aren't built for an iguana. I'm really only good on trees."

The poor thing. "Why don't you go rest then? If you think of anything anyone said or did, we can discuss it later."

"Okay."

As soon as Iggy waddled off, I returned my focus to the table, which was partially a mess. It appeared as if Armand had grabbed the table for support and ended up pulling down the plate of sugar cookies. Crumbs were everywhere, as was the broken plate they'd been served on.

"I'll look for a broom," Andorra said.

"Do you know if the sheriff's department bagged any of the food as evidence?"

"They did. I watched as they took a piece of everything."

That meant they hadn't discounted poison as a source of death. Good. While I wanted to grab one of the delicious-looking brownies, no telling who or what had touched them. "I guess I should toss it all."

"I would."

It didn't take as long as I'd expected to clean up since I just needed to dump the food into the trashcan. I kept the plates since some were really nice. Most likely, the neighbors assumed they would be picking their dishes up later.

After I cleaned the table and Andorra had swept and mopped the floor, I took the remaining dirty dishes into the kitchen to wash them.

We weren't halfway through when footsteps sounded behind us. "Glinda, Andorra, you don't have to do that."

Maddy had returned. I spun around. "We wanted to help."

"I appreciate that, but I could have done that."

"Nonsense, you need to rest. Let Jaxson or Drake get you a drink, and we'll finish up here."

"No. Just leave everything and come join us. We need to discuss what happened. Since you and Jaxson are amateur detectives, I'd love your input."

We couldn't do much to figure out what happened without the results of the autopsy. The sheriff needed to say if it was a natural death or not. Lastly, even if she said there had been foul play, we didn't know the dead man or any of the neighbors. Even if the sheriff asked for our help—which was doubtful— I didn't think we could do much. But hey. I had nowhere else to be. "Sure."

Drake and Jaxson both stood when we walked in. "Can I get you ladies anything?" Jaxson asked.

"Eugene can fix me a drink," Maddy said. "He knows what I like."

"I'll take a glass of wine." I hadn't had any before since I wanted to be on my best behavior.

"I'll have the same," Andorra said.

While Jaxson fixed us our drinks, I went into the bedroom where I found Iggy on the cot, seemingly asleep. I was sure that my sneaky little iguana had learned something, and I wanted to know what it was.

"You awake?" He was probably faking it.

When he didn't move, I tapped his head lightly. One eye opened. "Seriously?" he asked.

"We need your help."

"With what?"

I sat next to him. "You must have seen or heard something when you were at the party."

He lifted his chest. "Fine, but carry me into the living room. I'm not awake yet. I'll tell you and the others what I know, all at the same time."

Wasn't he being dramatic? After the day we'd had, I

didn't want to argue, so I picked him up. "Did you happen to talk with Hugo before he left?"

"He's gone?"

"All the guests left so I saw no need for him to stay around. Don't worry. I imagine we'll ask him to come back later tonight and fill us in."

"Good."

When I entered the living room with my familiar, Jaxson handed me a glass of wine, which was something I sorely needed. I sat next to him and asked him to hold Iggy so I wouldn't spill my drink.

"Dad, now that Glinda is here, go ahead."

"I'm thinking Armand might not have died on his own accord."

That was a bold statement. "You think he was murdered then?"

"Yes."

"How? He wasn't shot or stabbed. Are you thinking he could have been injected with something or eaten something poisonous?" I wasn't going to dismiss magic, but it was highly unlikely considering where we were and the fact that conducting a spell with everyone watching seemed highly unlikely.

"Any of those options are plausible. Armand was young and healthy. In fact, he ran marathons. Men like that don't just drop dead."

They did sometimes. I wonder if maybe he'd been allergic to an ingredient, like peanut butter. I doubt he would have dropped dead right away though. "Okay, I follow you so far. Who wanted him dead?"

"I don't know for sure, but here's my theory, and it's just that—a theory. The City Council is in a dilemma." He explained about the fairgrounds and how half of the Councilmen wanted to preserve it, while the other half wanted to tear it down.

"When I was in the dining room, I overheard Mary Jo Harper arguing with the deceased about it," I said.

"I'm not surprised. She's on the City Council and was convinced she could sway his vote. You see, there are only four members on the board. Two voted to keep the fairgrounds, and two wanted it torn down."

"If she could sway Armand's vote, her side would win. But why four members? Isn't it usually an odd number?"

Eugene nodded. "Yes, but one of the members became ill, and we've yet to replace him. That's why I was asked to step in. I'm the tie-breaker vote. I'm used in a limited capacity now, but I was a Council member for many years."

I wanted to be sure I understood. "Mary Jo was against the tear down while Armand was for it? Is that right?" Eugene nodded. "Who were the other voters?"

"Armand and Daniel Lee Jones were for the strip mall, whereas Mary Jo and Sharon Graeber were against it."

"And you?" He would be the deciding vote.

"I was the swing vote, but I couldn't let my opinion be known until after they were in deadlock for ten days."

That seemed arbitrary and very lengthy. "Which way would you have voted?"

"As much as I loved the fairgrounds, the equipment was in need of repair. I feared someone might be injured on the rides, so I would have voted to tear it down."

"It couldn't be fixed?" I asked.

"Old man Hargrove was too cheap to do it. He bought the land a long time ago and erected the fair. As the years went by, fewer and fewer attended, which meant he had less money to pour back into the business. He has a grandson, but I don't know if he's in any position to rebuild either, though I heard he is interested in taking over some day."

That was sad. "Could his grandson be behind this?"

"I don't know, but Graham wasn't at the party," Eugene said.

"That would be an issue unless he hired someone to *help* Armand meet his maker."

"No one here was a hitman," he said.

Well, someone probably killed him. I looked over at Jaxson and then back at his dad. "For the sake of argument, let's assume that murder was involved. It seems as if your killer was either Mary Jo or Sharon since they were for keeping the fairgrounds. They'd want to eliminate one of the tear down votes."

Eugene nodded. "True, but that would still end in a tie vote since I would have voted the same as Armand."

"Who would break the tie then?" Jaxson asked.

"The Mayor would provide the deciding vote. If I had to guess, he was leaning for keeping the fairgrounds."

My head spun. "If someone murdered Armand, you and Daniel Lee need to be careful."

"Don't worry about me. I'll stay put until this case is solved."

"Good." Iggy crawled over to my lap, and I looked down at him. "Did you hear something, my all-powerful iguana?"

"Yes. A bald guy wearing an ugly Christmas sweater was talking to a woman with kind of short hair. He didn't sound happy at all."

Not knowing anybody's name was going to a hindrance. I couldn't even guess who they were, though I do remember seeing an ugly sweater. "Go on."

"They were whispering. I would have gone over to them to eavesdrop, but it wasn't safe. They might have kicked or stepped on me."

"I'm glad you were careful. Thanks for trying." Okay that was a bust. I would have translated what Iggy said, but he really didn't know much. "Iggy didn't see much."

"I guess we can't do much more then." Jaxson's dad

slapped his thighs. "I know we usually wait until Christmas morning to open the gifts, but I think we can make an exception this year and open one present each. What do you all say? Today has been a little stressful."

I always liked presents, but it was up to the other Harrison members to decide. It was their tradition.

"Go for it, Dad," Jaxson said.

"I'm game," Drake said.

"Great." Eugene grabbed a bunch of gifts, one for each of us.

My present came from Drake. I tore it open and found a gift certificate to the Spellbound Diner. "This is perfect since we eat there almost every day. Thank you."

Drake smiled. "You're welcome."

Jaxson received a gift card from his mom that would allow him to load up on a few computer applications, and his dad gave his mom an apron, which I thought was a bit sexist, but she seemed really happy with it. I gave Andorra a gift card from the Moon Bay Nail Spa for a manicure and a massage.

"I love it. I never pamper myself."

"I know."

Drake gave his dad a bottle of scotch, and Drake received a month's worth of movie tickets. He loved the classics.

Maddy stood. "Thank you everyone for all of your support. I'm so sorry this had to happen when you guys were here. We hardly ever get together, and then when we do, we have a tragedy."

"Don't worry, Mom," Drake said. "We'll be sure to come back at a less hectic time."

She gave him a weak smile. "That would be great. I'm going to clean up and then go to bed. Tomorrow is a big day." She turned to Eugene. "Come join me."

He looked at us as if he wanted to stay and chat, but he seemed to realize his wife needed him more.

Once they left, the four of us gathered closer.

"I've been thinking," Jaxson said.

"You so stole that line from me." I pretended to act outraged.

"Guilty as charged, but here's what I propose. If, by the day after tomorrow, we don't learn that Armand Linfield was murdered, we drive back to Witch's Cove as planned. We'll celebrate Christmas with Glinda's folks, and you guys can share the holiday with Bertha, Elizabeth, and our two shifters."

"Don't forget Ruby," Andorra said.

I waited for Iggy to make a snarky comment about Ruby, but he said nothing. Andorra's cousin, Elizabeth, had more or less inherited the white cat familiar when a prominent woman in our community had died. This cat had special powers and had given Iggy superpowers for a day. His dislike of her had turned into something that resembled respect after that.

"Never," Jaxson said.

"Too bad Ruby hadn't come with us. I bet she might have learned something," I added. "People don't pay much attention to a cat—other than wanting to pet it."

"True," Andorra said.

Jaxson held up a hand. "Here's the rest of my plan, which could include Ruby if need be. If we find out that someone murdered Armand, we return and help with the investigation." He turned to Drake. "I know you have the wine shop to take care of, and you, Andorra, have to work at Hex and Bones, but if you want to help in any way—assuming the sheriff lets us—you should come back with us."

Drake nodded. "I'd like to. We don't need Dad to start nosing around and get in someone's crosshairs."

I wondered why Jaxson didn't mention involving Hugo and Genevieve. "Jaxson, didn't Andorra tell you that we invited Hugo and Genevieve to spy on everyone after we learned Armand was dead?"

"No."

"Sorry," Andorra said. "I kind of forgot."

"What did they learn?" he asked.

"That's what we need to find out. Want to join us in the bedroom? We don't need your parents walking in on two strangers."

"Absolutely."

CHAPTER FOUR

"I'll give Genevieve a call," Andorra said. "One lucky thing about those two is that they never sleep."

While Andorra dialed Genevieve's number, we made ourselves comfortable on the bed and cot. We motioned that she put the gargoyle shifter on speaker.

Genevieve answered right away. "Yes?"

"Did you learn anything when you were here?" Andorra asked.

Either Genevieve recognized Andorra's voice, or else she had caller ID on her phone. If I had to guess, Andorra had set it up for her.

"We did. Do you want us to come over?" she asked.

"All of us are in the bedroom where you first found me and Glinda."

"Okay."

Before Andorra could swipe off the phone, our two gargoyles appeared.

"Hugo!" Iggy perked up upon seeing his good friend.

Hugo immediately lifted Iggy and cradled him in his arms. The smile on Hugo's face said it all. He'd missed Iggy, too.

I turned to Genevieve. "What did you learn?"

She inhaled. "Hugo worked the living room, while I was in the dining room."

"Tell us everything," Andorra said.

"Well, I was moving around the room listening to a lot of conversations. One lady was commenting about the fact that Armand and his wife were arguing shortly before he died."

"Her name is Lydia." I thought it might be easier if we had names.

"Got it."

"Did the woman say what they were arguing about?" Drake asked.

"Yes. Lydia thought her husband was cheating on her with someone named Trixie. This same gossip lady was telling her friend that Lydia threatened to leave him if he didn't dump this Trixie chick."

I whistled. "That sounds like she was really mad." I pulled out my phone and made a note. "Doesn't it seem odd that Lydia would bring up such a delicate situation at a Christmas party where anyone could have heard her?"

"Some people can't control their emotions," Jaxson said.

That sounded logical. "Okay. Anything else?"

Genevieve looked over at Hugo. They did their silent communication exchange for a bit, and then she faced us. "Hugo heard Sid Harper tell his wife not to worry. That no matter what happened next, the vote would go her way. He'd make sure of it. I'm not certain what he was talking about, though," Genevieve said.

I explained about the City Council vote regarding whether to tear down the fair or not. I looked over at Jaxson. "Did Sid just confess?"

"Anything is possible, but my guess is that he was trying to be supportive to his wife. Sid had to realize that even with Armand dead, it wouldn't ensure a victory. My dad's vote would have had the same impact."

"Your dad said he hadn't leaked which way he'd vote."

Jaxson nodded. "I think his discretion is why my father has been re-elected so many times."

Out of habit, I raised my hand and then started talking without being called on. I forgot for a moment that I wasn't in school. "Question. If Mr. Hargrove owns the land that the fair is on, can the city really confiscate it?"

"I imagine if it's an eyesore, they can condemn it. I don't know much about eminent domain, though," Drake said. "I thought the city could buy a person's property if they had to put a road through it or something."

"I read that the city can buy the private property at fair market price and then sell it to a developer as part of an attempt to revitalize the town," Jaxson said.

"A strip mall would fit that bill," Drake said.

I blew out a breath. "That would stink for Mr. Hargrove."

"True that," Andorra mumbled.

"Anything else?" No one answered. "Thanks, Genevieve and Hugo. We really can't do anything at the moment. It's possible that Armand just dropped dead all by himself."

Jaxson dipped his chin. "It seems unlikely."

"I agree, but for now, our hands are tied. Tomorrow is Christmas. For your mom and dad's sake, let's pretend as if nothing has happened. The day after, we'll proceed according to your suggestion. We'll return to Witch's Cove and ask your father to call us if he learns anything."

"Sounds good," Drake said. "We'll enjoy Christmas and then regroup if need be."

Andorra turned to Genevieve and Hugo. "Thank you, guys. Drake and I will be home day after tomorrow. If you think of anything, make a note of it, and we'll discuss it when we get back."

"Sure thing."

Hugo handed Iggy back to me, and then they disappeared.

Drake shook his head. "I'm not used to them being here one moment, and then gone the next."

I smiled. "It takes a while to get used to it, not that I'm there yet."

Jaxson stood. "Mom will be making breakfast first thing tomorrow morning. I think she believes her little children will be sitting by the tree at six in the morning waiting for her and Dad."

I smiled. "That is endearing."

Jaxson tilted his head. "She needs to live in the present."

"Easier said than done."

"How well I know." Jaxson leaned over and gave me a quick kiss. "See you tomorrow morning."

"I wouldn't miss it." That meant I'd have to set my alarm, but it wouldn't be set for six, that was for sure.

Turns out, I didn't need an alarm for Christmas morning, because Iggy crawled onto the cot and tapped my face long before I was ready to get up—breakfast or no breakfast. I cracked open an eye. "Merry Christmas," I said with a very dry mouth.

"Shh. Andorra isn't up."

Are you kidding me? She was an early bird—at least compared to me. When my eyes adjusted to the light, I could tell it was barely dawn. "Why are you up?"

"I happened to wander into the living room a bit ago."

"Were you checking out the Christmas presents?" He better not have tried to open any. Even if he pawed at them, all he could have done was tear the paper.

"No! What do you take me for? I'm not a child."

"Fine. Then what was in the living room that has you so excited?" I asked.

"Pete."

"Who's Pete?"

"How could you forget him? He's the parrot who doesn't say much."

"Oh, yeah. I forgot his name for a moment." I dragged a hand over my eyes. "Don't worry. Pete is not a seagull. He will not poop on you."

Iggy nudged my arm. "I know, but Pete spoke to me."

"Pete talked yesterday. Didn't you hear him?"

"You aren't listening!"

Iggy was rarely this insistent. I propped myself up onto my elbows. "Okay. I'm almost awake. I'm ready to listen. Tell me."

"He's a familiar. He can talk like you and me."

Iggy was probably having Hugo withdrawals. "No

one is a witch or warlock in this family, so he can't be a familiar."

"I know that, but Pete told me that his former owner was a witch. Remember, they used to live in Witch's Cove. When the lady died, Jaxson's mom took him in. Pete's been very frustrated for the last twenty years since all he can do is repeat what others say."

I sat up. "Hold on. I still have brain fog. You're saying that Pete can actually talk?"

He slapped his claw on his snout. I guess it was similar to our face smack. "What have I been saying?"

This could be big. "Did you ask him if he knew anything about the possible murder?"

"Not yet. We were busy getting acquainted."

I picked up my phone. It wasn't even six. While it was way too early to rise, it was Christmas. "I'll get up and then talk to Pete. Thanks for letting me know."

"I'll wait for you in the living room." Iggy crawled down to the floor and slipped out of the room.

As soon as he was gone, I washed and dressed. Andorra would want to learn about this talking parrot, too. Before I left, I leaned over her bed. "Psst. Andorra. You awake?" Because her mouth was opened and her eyes were closed, I spoke softly.

She groaned, rolled over, and then opened her eyes. "What time is it?"

"Time to get up."

"Seriously?"

"Iggy just learned that Maddy's parrot is a familiar. He can talk."

She bolted upright. "What? How is that possible?"

I explained that Iggy learned that Pete had been a familiar before coming to live with the Harrisons.

"Whoa. I need to clean up. I'll be right out."

When I stepped into the living room, I could hear someone in the kitchen. That had to be Maddy making us breakfast. Before I woke up Jaxson and Drake, I wanted to speak with Pete. If he'd been able to hear every conversation over the years, he'd be a font of information.

I stepped up to the cage. "Hi, Pete. Iggy tells me you can talk."

"Don't tear it down."

That sounded like the opposite of what he'd said yesterday. It also sounded like something he'd heard. I stepped closer. "Iggy is my familiar, so feel free to talk."

Iggy looked up at me. "You didn't hear that?"

"Yes." I repeated what Pete said.

"No, after that."

"After that?"

Iggy glanced up at Pete, acting as if I'd lost it. "Pete, would you please repeat what you said. I'm sorry if Glinda wasn't listening."

His beak opened and shut, but nothing came out.

"Yes, Glinda is a witch," Iggy said to Pete. He then

faced me. "Pete doesn't understand why I can hear him, yet you can't."

I didn't think I was losing it. I snapped my fingers. "Remember when you could see that cat ghost and I couldn't?"

"Sure. Her name was Sassy."

"Yes. Maybe it's like that. When Ruby infused you with magical power—temporary that it was—maybe it came with some kind of residual effect."

"You mean I'm the only one who can understand Pete?"

"It could be. Andorra will be here shortly. She might be able to communicate with Pete, or maybe Jaxson can."

Iggy shook his head. "Pete said that since Jaxson isn't a warlock, they've never been able to communicate."

I explained how I'd put a spell on Jaxson so that he could understand Iggy. "You could try again, Pete. It would be cool if you two could talk with each other."

Pete nodded his head. He didn't have to speak for me to understand that action.

Andorra came out of the room, dressed in a cute red top and green jeans. She was definitely in the Christmas spirit. She went up to the bird cage. "Hi, Pete. I'm Andorra, Drake's girlfriend—and I'm a witch. Aren't you a beauty. I'll have to introduce you to my familiar. His name is Hugo."

"Hugo is a gargoyle shifter," Iggy added.

We waited for Pete to welcome Andorra, but he said nothing. Iggy turned to her. "Pete says, hi."

I looked over at Andorra who looked back at me. "Did you hear him?"

"No." I lifted Iggy. "Are you upset that Hugo left? Is that why you are saying that Pete can talk?"

Iggy bobbed his head, a sign he was upset. "No. Pete can talk. Just because I'm the only one who can hear him doesn't make it a lie."

His reasoning sounded like mine when I was trying to explain to others that Iggy could talk. "You're right. Maybe you're the only one who can hear him. How ironic!"

"What does that mean?" He glared at me.

"You and Pete have a connection. Pete is a bird. You don't like birds."

"I don't like seagulls."

Whatever. We must have made too much noise because the two brothers emerged from the hallway. "You're up early, Glinda!" Jaxson said.

I went into the reason for the early rising. Jaxson faced Pete. "You can talk?"

"Only I can communicate with him," Iggy said with a bit too much arrogance.

"Okay then." Jaxson placed a hand on my shoulder. "How about we let Iggy and Pete have a play date while the rest of us chow down? I'm starving, and my mom makes a mean breakfast."

"Great idea." I guess he didn't believe Iggy, not that I blamed him.

The four of us headed toward the dining room.

"Go to the fairgrounds," Pete called out. "Go to the fairgrounds."

I stopped. "I heard that."

"I did, too," Jaxson said. "But remember, Pete is a parrot. He picks up on conversations and repeats it. Nothing more."

"The more I think about it, the more I'm tending to believe Iggy. He doesn't lie—at least not often. If he said he can talk to Pete, then he can talk to Pete. If the parrot had been a familiar, then he might know what happened to Armand." Admittedly, he wasn't in the dining room at the time of the death, but if Eugene had members of the Council over to his house in the recent past, Pete might have heard a thing or two.

"We'll let Iggy pick Pete's brain, and then he can tell us everything."

"Perfect." Right now, the scent of coffee was drawing me to the table. Not only was there a delicious smelling pot of coffee, but Maddy had prepared a bowl of fruit and a plate of sweet rolls.

As soon as we sat down, she came out of the kitchen carrying a tray full of eggs and bacon. She looked up and smiled. "There he is."

Eugene came in with a smile on his face. "Merry Christmas, everyone."

If I hadn't been here yesterday and seen the dead body, I never would have known a tragedy had occurred. They acted as if it had never happened, and it might be for the best if I did the same.

CHAPTER FIVE

"I HATED that we left your parents to deal with all of that mess," I said. "I know they acted as if everything was back to normal, but I have the sense they are still on edge."

Jaxson glanced over at me right before he changed lanes on our way back to Witch's Cove. "They are definitely stressed, but I don't think having us under foot will help keep them any calmer. They need answers."

"I guess we can enjoy today with my family, and once we learn the details of Armand's death, we'll decide our next move." I twisted toward him. "Suppose your dad calls and says they did a toxicology screen on Armand and found he was poisoned. Then what?"

He blew out a breath. "We'll go back to my folks' place and start asking questions. It's what we do."

"Can we ask Hugo and Genevieve to come?" Iggy

asked.

"Hugo can't talk, but if he wants to stay close to Genevieve while she asks questions, I'm good with that."

"We could ask Elizabeth and Ruby too. Then you two can do another spell to make me all-powerful again," Iggy added.

My poor familiar. I wasn't sure if we repeated the spell that the result would be the same. "We'll see."

A little before dinner, we arrived in Witch's Cove. "I need to go home and clean up," Jaxson said. "How about I pick you up in an hour?"

"Perfect."

"Need help with the suitcase?" he asked.

Jaxson was such a good man. "I've got it."

Iggy and I went through the side door of the Tiki Hut Grill and then up the stairs to our apartment.

"I'm starving," Iggy said.

"I'll fix you something."

By the time I fed Iggy, unpacked, and cleaned up, Jaxson showed up.

"Ready to do our second Christmas?" he asked.

"Absolutely." Since Rihanna was with her boyfriend, Gavin, for the holidays—other than on Christmas morning—we'd exchanged gifts beforehand. I'd also had a small celebration with Aunt Fern. All that was left was to exchange gifts with my parents.

Iggy wanted to visit with Aimee, Aunt Fern's talking

cat, so we let him stay behind. I really think he didn't want to join us because of his issue with Toto, my mom's tiny dog, who'd scratched Iggy once.

We went next door to the funeral home since my parents lived above it and climbed the stairwell on the side of the building. I knocked and entered. I hadn't told my folks about the murder, so I imagined we'd be discussing it at some point.

"Hello?" I called out.

My father was the first to emerge from his den. "Glinda, Jaxson. Merry Christmas."

From the pots clanging, my mother was in the kitchen, preparing dinner. "Merry Christmas, Dad." We exchanged a light hug. "Does Mom need help?"

"Go see," he said.

The scent of the ham had my mouth watering. I couldn't believe my mother wanted to cook two Christmas meals. I wish I'd inherited her culinary talent, but it was not meant to be.

As soon as I entered the kitchen, my mom spun around and grinned. "You made it."

We hugged. "We did. What can I do to help?"

"The table is set, so how about carrying out the ham and potatoes."

We'd called ahead and given her our ETA, which was why the meal was all set to go. Once the food was on the table, we dug in.

"Tell me about your trip," Mom said. "And how were

Jaxson's parents?"

"I loved seeing them again, but there was a little snag."

"Oh?"

For the next half hour, Jaxson and I told them about the possible murder.

"What are you going to do?" my father asked.

"What can we do? We have to wait until we learn if Armand was killed. Even then, I'm not sure what we can do. We don't know the neighbors or the town. And the sheriff isn't exactly the overly friendly type." I snapped my fingers. "I got it. Mom, can you connect with the murdered victim, Armand Linfield? We could ask Andorra and Elizabeth to join us for a séance, but you are often more successful in contacting the deceased directly after the person passes."

She waved a fork. "I guess it's worth a try."

That was easy. "How about after we clean up and open the gifts, we see if Armand is willing to talk?"

"Perfect."

Then Mom and I discussed how Toto's health was doing. The Cairn Terrier had a few health scares in the last few months, but she seemed to be better now.

Once we finished eating, we went into the living room and put Dad in charge of passing out the presents. The exchange went quickly since Jaxson and I had already given each other our gifts.

I gave my mother some candles since she used a lot

of them when she communicated with the dead, as well as a book I'd found about the making of *The Wizard of Oz*. She was thrilled. For my dad, I gave him a new tie, some socks, and a mauve dress shirt. That might sound boring, but he liked to dress up every day when he met with the relatives of the deceased.

My folks gave Jaxson a nice navy blue sweater and me a deep maroon one. It wasn't quite pink, but it was in the red family.

After we chatted a bit more, Mom and I went downstairs to the conference room to contact Armand. Being the pro that she was, she quickly set up the candles and sprinkled a bit of sage on the table. She then wrote down his name, along with the questions I wanted to have answered.

"They rarely stay around for more than a minute or so," she said. "These should be more than enough."

Armand wouldn't appear or talk through a person, like in a séance, but my mother would *hear* him.

She lit the candles and closed her eyes. I knew my role—say and do nothing, and I was okay with that.

"Armand Linfield. I'm sorry you left us so unexpectedly. Did someone harm you?" She inhaled and nodded. "I see. Do you know who it was?"

I held my breath. I was hoping that my mother would say his answer out loud, but she didn't.

"Why would someone want you dead?" She seemed to be listening. "Can you narrow it down?" Her shoulders slumped, and then she opened her eyes. "He's gone."

I wasn't all that surprised. "What did he say?"

"He remembers that after arguing with his wife, he ate a cookie. Armand mumbled that it was a pink something. I couldn't catch that last word. He then felt a burning sensation, and his whole body shook. Before he could say or do anything, he blacked out. It happened really fast."

"Does that mean he was murdered?" I refused to believe Maddy had any connection to the man's death.

"He thinks so."

That was progress. "I take it he doesn't know who did it?" The newly dead were often in a state of confusion.

"No, but he said that being a Councilman had resulted in him having a lot of enemies."

"I can guess who two of them are." We'd briefly discussed the issue the Magnolia City Council was dealing with.

"I wouldn't draw any conclusions. It might have nothing to do with Council business. Someone might have tried to bribe him, and Mr. Linfield turned him down. That person could have wanted revenge."

My mom was guessing, but she often had good instincts. "That makes it even more difficult. Thanks for contacting him."

"You're welcome, sweetie."

It was times like these that it was helpful to have a witch for a mother. After we put everything away, we returned upstairs. Both Jaxson and my dad looked up.

"Anything?" Jaxson asked.

Mom told them what she'd heard. Jaxson's lack of follow up questions implied he understood that the contact hadn't yielded much.

We stayed for some coffee and dessert and then left, mostly because I was beat. It had been a mentally tiring day. Jaxson walked me back to my place. In case Iggy was inside, I wanted to have an uninterrupted kiss with my fiancé without some snarky comment from my familiar.

"We should do something special tomorrow. We don't have a case, and I don't feel like staying home alone," I said.

Jaxson wrapped his arms around my waist. "What is your pleasure?"

"It's a bit too cold to do the beach thing, but we could take in a museum?"

"Which one?"

"How about the Dali museum?" I'd been to it before, but I loved listening to the different docents' take on the man's life.

"Sounds like a plan. Call me when you get up."

"You bet."

We kissed goodnight, and then I went inside where Iggy was waiting for me. He insisted that I fill him in.

No surprise, he wasn't much interested in our presents, but he wanted to hear about my mom contacting Armand.

"I wish I had been there," Iggy said.

"Why?"

"Hello! I have super powers."

"You do."

Iggy was probably referring to his ability to speak with Pete, the parrot. I could have argued, but it was possible that it was all true. It had been a month since we'd done the spell that enabled my familiar to move through a solid object. When he tried the next day and failed, I assumed the spell had worn off, but maybe Ruby had given him—intentionally or not—other powers that had only now manifested themselves.

"I can tell you still don't believe me." Iggy turned around and crawled onto his stool.

At the moment, I wanted to change and relax in bed with a good book, not debate with Iggy. "No, I do. I wish you had been with my Mom and me, too, when we contacted him. Armand might have revealed more."

The museum visit was amazing, but I had the sense that Jaxon wasn't into it. "Is something wrong?" I asked as we returned to his truck.

"I didn't realize that waiting to hear from my dad

about the results of Armand's autopsy would have me on edge."

He was concerned about how his parents were handling this, and I couldn't blame him. I almost smiled at how much he'd grown. As a kid, Jaxson said he acted out in order to gain his father's attention. Now? He just wanted to keep both of them safe.

"It's Christmas. Maybe the medical examiner wants to be with his family," I said.

"He came to the house Christmas Eve," Jaxson said.

"Which might be why he wants to spend time with them now." Though if Elissa Sanchez had been the one to examine the body, she probably would have worked through the holiday and had a preliminary rcport by now. At the very least, she would have done a toxicology screen. The fact that they bagged the food implied they didn't want to discount foul play. "I assume you've called your dad?"

"I texted him. I didn't want to make him any more anxious than he already is."

I could understand that. "Just in case Armand was murdered, should we be proactive and attempt to fill out the white board?"

He shrugged. "We barely know anyone associated with the man. If the Councilman was murdered, we'll go to my folks and check it out. We can even toss the white board in the back if you like."

That made me happy. "Thank you."

Two days later, we were in the office tidying up when his dad contacted Jaxson. “Hey, Dad.”

With his cell in his hand, Jaxson got up from his desk, came over, and sat next to me on the sofa. I leaned in close so I could hear the conversation.

“Sheriff Waters called and said someone murdered Armand,” his dad said.

“That honestly doesn’t surprise me. Did she say how he died?” Jaxson asked.

“They think it was poison. The reason they aren’t sure is because the medical examiner couldn’t identify the drug in his system. He sent the sample off to a bigger lab.”

“Do you want us to come over?”

“What can you do?” his dad asked.

“It’s what Glinda and I do. She’s a witch and has some witchy friends. It’s amazing what a group of us can learn.” He looked over at me and raised his brows. I nodded.

“Your mother would probably feel better if you were here. She’s pretty upset. It’s a little late, but how about coming over around lunch tomorrow.”

“Can do. See you then.” Jaxson disconnected. “You heard all of that?”

“Yes. What do you think we can really accomplish, though? We tried filling out the white board, but I couldn't remember the names of those on the City Council let alone anyone else at the party."

"My folks will help the best they can. Plus, we can be supportive."

That went without saying. "Do you think Drake and Andorra will be able to join us?"

"Let me see what Drake wants to do. I imagine Andorra can take some time off even though we are in high season."

"What about Hugo, Genevieve, and maybe Ruby?"

He blew out a breath. "I don't think my folks are ready to meet two supernatural shapeshifters. As for Ruby, Mom is allergic to cats, but if we need Ruby's expertise, she could take her allergy pills."

Jaxson went downstairs to confer with his brother and didn't return for at least thirty minutes. When he came back upstairs, he gave me a thumbs up. "Drake and Andorra will ride with us."

"Great. And our two special friends?"

"They will be on standby. Genevieve can be with you girls at night if she wants, and Hugo can bunk with Drake and me."

Since they didn't sleep, neither would need a bed. "If we're leaving early, I better pack and then hit the hay."

"Pick you up at eight? We can stop on the way for some breakfast."

I inwardly groaned. "You bet."

CHAPTER SIX

"Your whiteboard is a great idea," Eugene said.

"Thanks, but we need help filling it out," I said.

"I have a list of those who came to the party. I'll get it." Maddy stood and went into another room.

"Dad, what exactly did the sheriff tell you?" Jaxson asked. "I know she can be a bit tight-lipped."

"You think? All she would say was that Armand had one undigested cookie in his stomach. Unfortunately, it was the sugar cookie with the pink frosting that your mom baked."

Drake's eyes opened. "The sheriff doesn't think Mom poisoned Mr. Linfield, does she?"

His dad huffed out a breath. "It's possible, but Sheriff Waters said she isn't pointing a finger until the results come back from the lab."

"If Maddy had laced the cookies with poison, more

people would have died. I know for certain that this short chunky man grabbed one." I turned to Jaxson. "What was the name of the man I was talking to when you saved me."

"Mr. Eberhart."

"Wilson is my neighbor," Eugene said. "I think he's still alive. Or at least, I hope he is. How about I give him a call and find out?"

"That would be great, Dad," Jaxson said.

Just as his father contacted Mr. Eberhart, Maddy returned and handed us the guest list. "I made some notes as to who was a Councilmember, who they were married to, and who had other jobs. Quite a few are retired."

I smiled. "This is really helpful. Thanks."

Eugene disconnected. "Turns out that Wilson did grab a pink sugar cookie, but that when Jaxson came in, he was a bit flustered and set it down."

"He didn't eat it?" I know that was what his father had said, but I wanted to be sure.

"No."

Maddy's hand shook. "I did not put poison in my cookies. Glinda, you or anyone else could have eaten one."

Poor woman. "I know. I'm sure the sheriff will figure it out."

"Jane is good, Maddy," Eugene said. "I trust her."

Jaxson pointed to the paper in my hand. "Glinda,

how about I read off the names and you write them down on the board?"

"Perfect."

"Dad and Mom, try to suggest why someone might want Armand dead. Glinda and I like to give each person a rating from one to ten as to how likely it is this person could be the killer, with ten being the most likely they are guilty."

"We can do that," his father said.

Iggy was on the coffee table, absorbing it all. "We need Pete to help, too," he said.

I glanced over at the bird who was nodding frantically. "What does Pete want to do?"

"He wants to help."

I told them what Iggy said.

Maddy chuckled. "How can our parrot help?"

Jaxson leaned back in his chair. "I need to tell you all something."

"What's that?" his father asked.

"Turns out, his original owner was a witch."

"Mrs. May was a witch? That's ridiculous," Maddy said.

"Why?" I asked. "I'm a witch with a familiar who can talk."

Andorra nodded. "I can hear Iggy but not Pete, but I believe that Iggy can communicate with him."

Maddy looked over at her husband. "Glinda, my son

mentioned that you'd put some kind of spell on him that enables him to hear Iggy. Is that right?"

"Yes."

"But you can't hear Pete?" Eugene asked.

"Only Iggy can," I said. "I don't know why that is though."

Iggy looked over at me. "You know why. I'm special. To prove it everyone, let's do that guess-the-number trick to show them."

That stunt was hokey, but if we were going to solve this crime, we needed all the help we could get. "Sure."

"What did he say?" Maddy asked.

"Iggy wants to prove to you how smart he is and that we can communicate. I know you believe me, but Iggy likes doing his parlor tricks when he can."

"I'm game," Maddy said.

I picked up a pen, retrieved the list of names from Jaxson, and handed both to Maddy. "On the back, write down a number—any number. When I turn around, show the number to Iggy. He'll then tell me, and I'll tell you."

"He can read?"

"Yes." I didn't need to list his many talents.

"Okay." She sounded hesitant, and I could understand why. I stood and faced away from her.

The pen scratched on the paper. "She wrote seven hundred and forty-three," Iggy said. "From the smirk on her face, I don't think she believes I can do this."

We could discuss that later. “Maddy, you wrote seven hundred and forty-three.” I turned around.

Maddy’s mouth opened. “How?”

“It’s magic.”

“Well, I’ll be. That’s incredible.” Maddy looked over at Iggy. “You are one smart lizard.”

Iggy bobbed his head. To non-witches, it was his way of saying thank you.

“Now about Pete,” I said.

Jaxson stood. “I’ll let him out.”

He removed Pete from his cage and placed him on the coffee table. I hoped he understood that he needed to be good and not fly around or distract others.

Iggy faced Pete. “Here’s the deal. We’ll go over the names of possible suspects and give them a ranking from one to ten. One means we think it is highly unlikely— Oh, yeah. I forgot. You heard Glinda tell everyone what to do. Sorry.”

I was pleased that Iggy had been paying attention to my grading system. “What did Pete say?” I asked.

“He’ll help when he can.”

“Great.”

“Glinda?” Eugene asked.

It was really tiring having to translate all the time. I wish I knew of a spell that would allow others to understand familiars, even if it was only for a few days. I looked over at Andorra and an idea struck me. “This will sound crazy, but is there any way Hugo could do some kind of mental mumbo jumbo that will allow all of us to hear Pete and Iggy? Even if for a short while, it would speed things up."

She shrugged. "I can ask."

"Who is Hugo?" Maddy asked.

This would be hard to explain. "Jaxson, do you want to do the honors?"

He inhaled deeply. "I'll try. Hugo is Andorra's familiar, but when he and his friend get here, I'll explain in more detail. It's a bit complicated."

"Are they like Iggy and Pete?" Maddy asked.

"No. They look like us. As I said, it's complicated."

Andorra called Genevieve.

"Tell her to wait a bit before leaving," I mouthed.

Andorra nodded. She explained about needing their expertise. "But we need you guys to—" Andorra's head dropped back, and she let out a breath.

I had been cut off many times before when I'd spoken with Genevieve, so I understood what probably just happened. I looked around. "Genevieve and Hugo, I assume you are here. If so, you might as well show yourself and shock the Harrisons all at once."

They instantly appeared, and Maddy grabbed Eugene's hand. "Glinda, what just happened?"

"Mom and Dad, meet Genevieve Dubois and Hugo. Hugo is mute, but Genevieve is not. They are here to help," Jaxson explained.

"How did they get here? They didn't even knock. The front door didn't open."

For the next twenty minutes, we tried to explained how they came to be and what and who they were. Until Jaxson's parents witnessed their talents, I'm not sure they could fully understand the extent of their abilities.

I turned to Hugo and explained our need for everyone to be able to hear Iggy and Pete, even if it was only for a day or two. "Can you do that?"

Hugo walked over to Jaxson. I thought that was a good first choice. He stood behind him, placed his hands on either side of Jaxson's head, and then did his own kind of magic.

When Hugo lowered his arms, Jaxson spoke to Pete. "Give me your best shot." A few seconds later, Jaxson's arms rose. "I can hear him." He turned around and grinned. "Thank you, Hugo."

Hugo smiled briefly and then moved from one person to the next. I was impressed that Maddy and Eugene didn't object when it was their turn, nor did they question what Hugo was doing. It was so great that they had such trust in their son.

When Hugo finished, Iggy waddled across the table to face Jaxson's parents. "Hi, I'm Iggy."

They looked at each other, but it was Eugene who answered. "Nice to meet you, Iggy."

The bird squawked to get everyone's attention. "Okay, everyone, I've been waiting twenty-years to talk to you guys. I don't know how long this mojo stuff will last, so I need to say my fill." Pete puffed out his chest and ruffled his feathers.

We all laughed. I could only imagine what it would be like to be silent for so long. While Pete told his owners a few things about his life in the cage, Iggy came over to me and crawled up my leg. "I'm not special anymore."

I figured that would bother him. Before, he had been the only one who could hear Pete, and now we all could. "You are the most special one of all."

"Why is that?"

"Because you're the most experienced one around familiars and such."

He turned his gaze away from me. "I guess."

Jaxson lightly clapped his hands together once. "Since we now can communicate with each other, how about we begin?"

I placed Iggy back on the coffee table and stood, ready to take notes on the whiteboard. "Like we said, Hugo is mute, but he can hear what we say. If he has an observation from the time he was here before, he'll use telepathy to tell Andorra or Genevieve, who will tell us."

"Or me," Iggy said.

I smiled. "Or you."

"He was here before?" Maddy asked.

I explained why we hadn't told them. "We didn't

want you to freak out."

"That was probably wise."

"Good. Now I'll write down the names that Maddy provided me, and then we'll take them one at a time." I started with Mary Jo Harper. "What would be her motive for killing Armand?" I could guess, but it would better if Eugene told us his opinion.

Jaxson's dad inhaled. "I think it's clear. She didn't want the fairgrounds to be torn down."

"Good. How would you rate her likelihood of being the killer?" I asked.

"Even though Armand's death might not have changed the Council's vote, she might not have known that. So I'd give her an eight."

I thought that was a bit high, but we could always change the number later. "What about her husband, Sid? Would he be capable of killing someone? Would he murder in order for his spouse to win this battle?"

"I can't say I know him all that well. I work with Mary Jo, not Sid. He does seem devoted to his wife, so give him a four," Eugene said.

Maddy grabbed Eugene's hand. "Do you really think Sid could bake a cake and put poison in it?"

"Mom," Drake said. "I don't think they found any cake in Armand's stomach. That aside, let's assume Mary Jo made that pink cake. I don't think it would take much to sprinkle some rat poison on top."

She pursed her lips. "This is all so tragic."

We didn't need to get sidetracked. "It is. Next is Sharon Graeber. I believe you said she was the other Councilwoman who was against tearing down the fairgrounds? Her husband is Clive."

After a short discussion, we decided that she should get a seven ranking since she wasn't as aggressive as Mary Jo. As for Clive, it was the same motive as Mary Jo's husband.

"That covers those who were against tearing down the fairgrounds. Anyone else who had a motive for killing Armand?"

"You need to find out who Trixie is," Genevieve said. She repeated what she'd heard during the party.

Eugene leaned closer. "We have a Trixie's diner. Do you think that's what Lydia was referring to?"

"No, his wife was definitely accusing the dead guy of having an affair with this Trixie woman."

"I can see we need to do a little research into her identity," Eugene said. "Definitely put Lydia down as a possible suspect then."

"Her motive would be jealousy, right?" I asked.

"Yes," Eugene said. "Give her an eight."

"Lydia was definitely angry," Genevieve interrupted. "We should give her at least a six."

An eight was bigger than a six, but I decided not to give her a math lesson.

"I disagree," Maddy said. "Lydia was so sad when Armand died. She couldn't stop crying."

"She could have been a good actress, or maybe she only meant to make him sick," I said. "I'm just trying to keep an open mind."

Maddy nodded. "I can see that. I honestly didn't know her all that well."

That seemed to be a theme here.

Genevieve turned to Hugo and nodded. Then he disappeared—without Genevieve.

"Where did he go?" Andorra asked.

"He thought it would be a good idea to check up on Lydia to see how she's doing," Genevieve said.

That sounded more like spying. "What is he expecting to find? Does he think she'll be having a party with some new boyfriend now that her husband is dead?" I usually wasn't that blunt, but I wanted to be totally aboveboard.

She shrugged. "Hugo doesn't know what he'll find, but he'll report back."

"How does he know where Lydia lives?" Maddy asked.

"He...uh...read your mind?" Genevieve said and then lowered her gaze.

Okay, that was rather invasive. Maddy's hand over her mouth implied she thought so too.

"I hope it was when he was giving everyone the powers to understand our familiars," I said.

"It was."

I wasn't sure that made it much better. "I hope he

doesn't go around doing that kind of mind reading willy-nilly," I said.

Genevieve sat up straighter. "No, and I told him not to do that again."

"Good," I said.

Hugo appeared. "That was fast," I said.

Genevieve listened, nodded, and then turned to us. "Hugo said that Lydia is putting her husband's possessions into garbage bags."

"She's not giving herself much time to grieve, is she?" I hadn't personally experienced a lot of death in my immediate family, other than my grandmother's, but it took my mom a long time to clean out her mother's house.

"I find that hard to believe," Maddy said. "Lydia should be in mourning."

"Hugo, was she crying or sniffling or anything to indicate she was grieving?" I wasn't sure if he knew what grieving was, but maybe he did.

He shook his head. I didn't want to ask if she was laughing and cheering. "Did she call anyone during the short time you were there?"

Once more he shook his head.

If I had to point a finger, I might think Armand's own wife had done him in.

CHAPTER SEVEN

NEXT, we talked about Daniel Lee being a suspect in Armand's murder. While he had voted in favor of tearing down the fairgrounds, he might have argued with Armand in the past about something else.

"Eugene," Pete said and then stilled. "I may call you that, right?"

Jaxson's dad almost smiled. "Yes, that's fine. No need to be formal after twenty years."

We all chuckled.

"This Daniel Lee man came to dinner one time, and Armand came, too, right?" Pete asked.

"He did, but it was a few months ago."

"I only heard you guys when you were having a drink out here in the living room, but he was not a happy guy."

Eugene glanced over at Maddy. "What do you think? I'm not as intuitive as you are."

"I agree with Pete. He seemed a bit distracted." She turned to her parrot. "Why do you ask?"

"Was he distracted because he was unhappy or angry with the dead guy for some reason?"

Eugene crossed his arms. "He never said anything during a Council meeting that I attended, but I didn't go to many of them. Remember, I was just an alternate."

"There's no obvious motive for Daniel Lee wanting Armand dead, but that doesn't mean he didn't do it," I said. "How about assigning him a two?"

Everyone nodded.

"Why not the fairground owner?" Pete suggested.

"Jack Hargrove has to be eighty. Besides, he wasn't at the party," Maddy said.

"Too bad. He had the best motive of them all," Drake said.

I nodded my agreement. "I'd be mad if the city was trying to take away my property. It doesn't matter if they gave me above market price."

"All the more reason we should at least talk to him. A different perspective is always helpful," Drake said.

"I bet Jane has already picked his brain," his dad said.

Jaxson turned to me. "Why don't we check it out tomorrow? We can take Iggy, and he can do his shouting-behind-the-guy's-back thing."

"You think Jack Hargrove could be a warlock?" I asked.

"Why not? We had no idea that our neighbor had been one."

"Agreed. I'm game." I know Iggy would be happy to be part of the case.

"I have an idea," Drake said.

"Yes?" Drake was always level-headed.

"It seems to me that we need to find this Trixie woman. She could tell us who Armand thought wanted him dead—assuming he was even aware he had a target on his back."

"His wife would be the most likely suspect," I said. "We should talk to her too."

"Glinda," Maddy said. "If she had nothing to do with Armand's death, it would be best to leave her be for a while."

For now, I'd agree. The sheriff would question her quickly so that she couldn't get rid of evidence if she were guilty. "Okay."

"What can I do?" Pete asked.

That was a good question. "Do you have any skills?"

"I can't read like Iggy can, because no one taught me. I was pretty young when Mrs. May passed, but I can cloak myself, and I can fly." He looked over at Iggy. "Can you fly?"

Whoa. Iggy already had issues with birds. The last

thing we needed was for the two of them to go head to head. "No, he can't, Pete, but just last month, he was able to move through wood."

Pete's ruffled feathers returned to their calm state. "Impressive."

Good. Immediate threat averted. I turned to Jaxson's parents. "Is there a diner around here, or a restaurant, where the locals might be willing to share some gossip?"

"Like I said, we have Trixie's," Eugene said. "It's small, and Viola is a chatterbox. She's the new owner."

That sounded promising. "Maybe Jaxson, Drake, Andorra, and I could eat dinner there. Someone must have heard about Armand's death."

"Sounds good, and I'll take Maddy out to a different place and ask around. If we spread out, we can cover more ground."

"Genevieve," Andorra said. "I realize you and Hugo don't need to eat, but how about staying cloaked so you can listen in on any gossip." She turned to Maddy. "Do you have a third suggestion for where they should go?"

"We have a malt shop on Main street."

"Great. I'm sure these two can find it."

And yes, one second they were there and the next they weren't. Andorra once more gave the Harrisons a rundown of her familiar and his impetuous girlfriend.

Once we wrapped up the suspect list, we each

headed to our assigned areas. Ours was to check out the fairgrounds, while Drake and Andorra would snoop downtown until it was time for dinner.

When we pulled up into the fairground's parking lot, my heart sank. The last fair we'd attended had been in Ohio, and this was nothing like that one. The Ohio fair had a huge Ferris wheel, a ton of booths that served food, and several side shows in large tents.

In contrast, the equipment looked a little worn, and the faded awnings on the closed food trucks implied a general lack of upkeep. Because Christmas was not an optimum time to have a fair, it was closed until March —or so said the rather decrepit sign.

"Do you really think we're going to find Jack Hargrove here? I don't see any cars."

"Probably not, but as long as we're here, how about we look around?" Jaxson suggested.

"It's fenced in." I should have expected it would be since insurance companies would insist on it.

Once Jaxson cut the engine, I slipped out, and a cold breeze whipped across my face. This part of Florida was definitely chillier than Witch's Cove. It might have been more tolerable if the sun had been out.

"That lock looks like it might not be closed," Jaxson said. "Let me check it out."

"We can't just break in."

"It's not breaking in, if it's not locked." Jaxson tugged on the lock and it sprung open. "See?"

"Fine." We went inside, and I looked around. "Considering the state of things, I wonder why Mary Jo and Sharon pushed so hard to keep this place around?"

"Excellent question. Maybe they wanted to keep some good memories alive."

"I'd love to talk to the ladies, but I know GI Jane would not approve. I bet she'd say it was her investigation, not ours, and that she didn't need our help."

Jaxson chuckled. "That's the best case scenario. She might arrest us for interfering in a murder investigation."

"Let's hope magic is not involved. Otherwise, she'll be in way over her head," I mumbled.

We walked around the many acres for a good twenty minutes. Even though I knew little about mechanics, I was smart enough to realize that I would never get on one of the rollercoasters or any other piece of equipment that had moving parts. "I'm surprised Mr. Hargrove could get insurance on this place."

"Dad said he did last year, but I believe his policy is up for renewal the first of the year."

"If the owner can't get insurance, then the City Council's vote wouldn't matter."

"I bet they are hoping that's the case. It gives them a clearer conscious and makes it an easier sell to the towns' people."

"I guess."

"But if we find out who the inspector is, we should

warn him that his life might be in danger," Jaxson said. "Whether it would be from Hargrove himself or from the likes of Mary Jo Harper, I don't know."

"I bet the inspector has probably figured out that if the city wants the land for their own good. They'll find a reason to take it. His inspection report might not matter."

Jaxson's eyebrows rose. "Aren't we cynical today?"

"Maybe I am."

He was smart not to push it any further. Instead, Jaxson surveyed the area. "I don't see anyone around. Let's head back."

Once outside the gate, Jaxson secured the lock. Before we reached our truck, another vehicle pulled into the parking lot. We slowly moved toward our truck, waiting for the occupant to emerge. The driver was around eighty, had wild white hair and a scruffy beard. His jeans looked like they could use a wash, and his jacket had seen better days. "Do you think that's the owner?"

"Only one way to find out. Mr. Hargrove?" Jaxson shouted.

The man stopped and waited for us to reach him. "Yes, I'm Jack Hargrove."

Since Jaxson's dad was on the City Council, I figured it would be best if Jaxson led the questioning. We introduced ourselves as Eugene Harrison's son and future daughter-in-law. It would be best if we didn't say that we were amateur sleuths.

"May we ask you a few questions?" Jaxson asked.

"About?"

"About why so many people want to tear down this city treasure and put up a strip mall? It's not as if the town doesn't have enough of them." For effect, Jaxson shook his head in apparent disgust.

I had to hand it to him. He knew how to soften up the guy.

"Sure. I have a little trailer in back. We can talk there. Besides, it will be warmer inside."

After he unlocked the gate, we followed him to the back of the fairgrounds. He might bc old, but once he started moving, he was rather spry. The inside of the trailer was a mess to put it mildly. If his maintenance skills were anything like his trailer, I wouldn't trust anything this fair had to offer.

He motioned we sit on the rather ratty looking sofa. "What do you want to know?"

Jaxson nodded to me. "I'm sure you've heard that Armand Linfield was murdered?"

"I did."

I waited for him to make a comment that indicated he was happy or sad about the death, but the man kept a neutral face. "Could you guess who might have wanted him dead?" I asked.

Jack dragged a hand down his unshaven chin. "Can't say that I do. That being said, I'm not sad that the Councilman who wanted to shut this place down can't vote no more."

Any more. I always mentally corrected people, which was not very polite, but once a teacher always a teacher. It didn't matter I taught math and not English. "Why do you keep the fairgrounds open? Is business that good?"

He barked out a laugh. "No. It's the land that I want to keep, and it's the land the city wants to take away from me, but I need to give my grandson something to remember me by."

"Not your children?"

"Ain't got none. My son drank himself to death. I only have Graham left. He's a good boy. He'll use the land for the right purpose." Jack lifted his chin with pride.

Jaxson leaned forward. "You aren't planning to open the fair again?" The sign might not have been up-to-date.

"Not anytime soon. The rides need a lot of work to make them safe, and I don't have that kind of money. I'm hoping Graham will take over soon and do what needs to be done."

I'd set my purse on the trailer floor as soon as we sat down. From the movement inside, Iggy had cloaked himself and was crawling out.

"I want to go on a ride," Iggy shouted.

I was glad he understood that Jack Hargrove could be hard of hearing. Regardless of Iggy's volume, the man didn't respond. Either he was nearly deaf, or he wasn't a warlock. If I had to guess, I'd say it was the latter. We weren't in Witch's Cove, after all.

While the owner seemed okay with having to close, he had to have some idea who was a champion of the fair remaining open, and who wanted him to sell.

"Who are your biggest supporters?" I asked.

"That's easy. There are two Councilwomen who have promised to have my back."

"Mary Jo Harper and Sharon Graeber."

"That's them. As a matter of fact, Mary Jo's husband, Sid, offered to be my partner in order to keep the fair alive, but I turned him down. I don't trust anyone but family. Sid seems like a slick one, if you know what I mean. They'll tell you one thing and then do another."

"I'm sorry." I was surprised that Eugene knew none of this. "Did anyone other than the city try to buy the land from you for something other than the strip mall? Like was anyone interested in keeping it as a park for the town's residents?"

I was curious why he didn't sell the property and give the money to his grandson after he passed. Money might be more welcome than land. Or was Mr. Hargrove against strip malls in general?

He scratched his chest. "Can't say I recall."

Really? Most likely he didn't want to tell us too much.

"I'm ready to go," Iggy said. Naturally, he expected us to leave immediately. I was fine with that since I didn't think Mr. Hargrove had much to add.

I looked over at Jaxson. "Anything else?"

"That's it for now."

We both stood, thanked Mr. Hargrove for his time, and left. As soon as we were out of earshot, I spoke up. "Something is off here."

"Why is that?" Jaxson asked.

"I wish I could put my finger on it. If this fair was amazing, clean, and safe, I could understand why Mary Jo and Sharon wanted it to be here for future generations. But it's not, so why are they so adamant about keeping it around, especially if Mr. Hargrove might never reopen."

"That is an excellent question. If we learn the answer to that, we might figure out who killed Armand."

I wasn't as hopeful, but it was worth a try. Tonight, when the four of us went out to dinner, it would be something to bring up to the server.

Upon returning to the Harrison home, I was happy to see everyone had returned from their initial assignment. "Hey, guys. I hope you all had a successful outing," I said.

Genevieve raised her hand. “We did.”

After taking off my light jacket and letting Iggy out of my purse, I dropped onto the sofa. “Tell us.”

“Hugo remained cloaked so he could move about freely, but I talked to some locals about the fairgrounds.”

“And?” I was fully aware that Genevieve was a long-winded story teller.

“Did you know that the fairgrounds was a real cool place to go at night when you were in high school?”

How would I know that since I’d never been to Magnolia before? “Can’t say that I did. How does this relate to Armand’s death?”

Genevieve shrugged. “I’m not sure, but if the city puts in a mall, then the kids won’t have a place to go.”

That was a real stretch, but I knew not to discount it just yet. “Did you hear it used to be a place for illicit activities?”

“Do you mean drinking and stuff?”

And stuff. “Yes.”

“I don’t know.”

Okay, maybe that was a bust. I looked over at Hugo. “You got anything, big guy?”

He faced Genevieve. I glanced at Andorra, his host. She used to be the one to translate. I wonder how she felt about being pushed aside.

“Hugo overhead some guy say that the poison that

killed Armand came from a local factory," Genevieve said.

That sounded intriguing. "Eugene, what kind of factories are near here?"

"A pesticide company. And guess who works there?"

CHAPTER EIGHT

I SAT UP STRAIGHTER. This could be the big clue. "Who works at a pesticide factory?"

"Sid Harper, Mary Jo's husband," Eugene said.

"I know this is jumping to conclusions, but could he have gotten a hold of a poisonous chemical and somehow sprinkled it on one of the cookies?"

Eugene shrugged. "If he did, I hope it was tasteless."

"It would make more sense if Sid poisoned his wife's cake and then suggested that Armand try a piece before anyone else did," I said.

Maddy leaned back in her chair. "I agree, but the fact is that Armand only ate one of my cookies. Is it possible, Sid poisoned the whole batch somehow?"

"I don't think so," I said. "It would be odd if Sid insisted Armand eat one of your cookies instead of his wife's cake. And that makes me think something else is at play here—or rather that Sid might not be guilty."

Jaxson leaned forward. "Hugo, did you hear if this poisonous chemical was solid or liquid?"

Hugo shrugged his shoulders.

"Why would it matter, bro?"

"What if someone injected Armand with the chemical. His cookie eating might have nothing to do with anything."

I shook my head. "He'd feel a needle sting and say something."

"Maybe he couldn't say anything. Did the sheriff mention if the poison paralyzed him by any chance?" Jaxson asked.

"Jane Waters reveals nothing during an ongoing investigation," Eugene said.

Good thing I didn't live in this town. The Pink Iguana Sleuths company would end before it began. "That's it!"

"What's it?" Jaxson asked.

"I didn't think it meant anything at the time, but remember when Mom contacted Armand?"

"Yes."

"How did she do that?" Maddy asked. "Armand is dead."

I could see why she'd be confused. I told her about my mother's abilities and then what Armand said.

"That seems like he was jabbed with a needle,"

Eugene said.

"Exactly. The burning sensation could be the poison going into his system. He said he couldn't say anything before he passed out," I reminded them.

"It fits. Maybe I can urge the Mayor to call Jane and ask her for information," Eugene said.

"That would be great." For some reason, I didn't think Jane Waters would bow even to the Mayor. "Moving on, which of you were in the room when Armand fell?"

"I was with you in the living room," Jaxson responded.

"Drake and I were in the living room too," Andorra said.

Maddy held up her hand. "I was in the kitchen getting another plate of desserts."

"And Genevieve and Hugo arrived after Armand died. I'd heard Armand arguing with his wife, but that was a while before he passed."

"I was there," Eugene said, "but I was talking with a neighbor. I didn't see anything though."

Well, that stinks. "The sheriff didn't happen to mention if this chemical was in his bloodstream or in his stomach, did she?" That would make a difference.

"Jane Waters might know, but like I said, she's not going to say anything without a court order."

Iggy! He was in there. "Iggy?"

"Don't look at me. You didn't let me go undercover

until after the guy died."

I slumped back. "That's true, and Pete was in his cage." He was now on the table with Iggy. I turned to him. "Did you overhear anything? You must have heightened senses."

"I do, but it's hard when everyone is talking."

"I get it. Well, from now on, keep your ears open."

Pete cocked his head. "In the house? I need to get out. Investigate. Be like Iggy here."

I'd let the Harrisons handle that one.

"Pete," Eugene said. "We appreciate your enthusiasm, but you've not left the house in twenty years. It's a hostile environment out there."

He looked over at Hugo. "I can go with the big guy here."

"Pete," Jaxson said. "Right now, we have it handled, but if your talents are ever needed, we'll call on you."

Pete bobbed his head. Either it meant he agreed or else he was upset. "Andorra and Drake? Did you two learn anything while you were out and about today?"

"Not a lot. I asked our server at the coffee shop whether she had heard about Armand's death, and she kind of rolled her eyes," Drake said. "Magnolia is a lot like Witch's Cove, implying of course, she had."

"What did she say?" I asked.

"Andorra made a comment about how sad it must be for his wife to have lost her husband, and our server kind of harrumphed."

"Implying what? That she didn't think Lydia was actually sad?"

"That's what I'm thinking," Drake said.

"Let Hugo and me spy on Lydia some more," Genevieve piped up.

Three of us answered at the same time, telling her to stay put, but alas, they were gone.

"Do they always just up and leave like that?" Maddy asked.

"Yup."

"Lydia won't know they are there, will she?" Eugene asked.

Of all the times we've worked with them, they'd never lost their ability to remain cloaked. "She won't know."

We chatted a bit more about anyone else who might have wanted Armand dead, but not knowing the method of his death hampered our ability to proceed.

I checked my cell phone for the time. It was close enough to dinner for us to grab some grub. "Are we ready to pick some more brains, assuming Andorra and Drake aren't full from their last meal?"

"We're good. We only had a coffee and a muffin," Drake said. "I even know where Trixie's restaurant is located."

I could only hope the owner or someone at the restaurant was willing to chat. "What are you two going to do?" I asked Jaxson's parents.

"I thought we'd visit Wilson. I'll take over a bottle of scotch and share a drink."

"Do you think he knows something, Dad?" Drake asked.

"Wilson? Why he's the biggest gossip of them all."

"Great. See if he knows who Trixie is since Genevieve is sure she was Armand's *other* woman."

Eugene gave us a thumbs up. After the four of us freshened up, we jumped in the truck and headed to town. Even though it was close to dark, I could appreciate how cute the downtown was. Jaxson parked close to the restaurant, and we all headed inside.

I was surprised to find that Trixie's was a fish restaurant, since the name didn't fit its theme. However, they'd done a nice job decorating it with many nautical items even though Magnolia wasn't on either of the two Florida coasts. I especially liked the images of the lighthouses and the fish nets that dotted the walls.

We were shown to a table near the back of the restaurant. Good. It might be easier to have a discussion with a server if we were out of earshot of the other guests.

A portly older woman with kind eyes came over to see what we wanted to drink. Her name tag read Viola. Yes! The owner. After we ordered our beverages, I slipped it in that we were here to find out about Armand Linfield's death.

"Such a shame, but between you and me, I'm not surprised."

This sounded encouraging. "Why not?"

Viola leaned over. "He was a ladies' man. I wouldn't be surprised if some jealous lady did him in."

Like his wife? Neither Maddy nor Eugene mentioned Armand's penchant for women. "He is married, you know."

"That didn't seem to matter to him."

This was getting better and better. "Was Mr. Linfield seeing Trixie on the side?" Yes, that was a stab in the dark, but we had nothing to lose.

Her eyes widened. "I believe that was her name, but she has no connection to this restaurant, mind you. Our namesake passed away years ago. When I bought the place, I decided not to change the name to Viola's." She scrunched up her nose. "That doesn't sound like a place you'd want to eat, now does it?"

"I like it." That was a very noncommittal answer, if I do say so myself.

Viola's brow furrowed. "If you're not from here, how did you know about Mr. Armand and Trixie?"

"Lucky guess."

"Do you know Trixie's last name?" Andorra asked.

She shook her head.

"Can you describe her?" Drake asked.

Viola shrugged. "It's hard to say, because he was in here with several different women. I think he worked with many of them, judging by their conservative attire."

"Trixie didn't stick out in any way?" Having been a waitress, I made it a point to remember something about each customer in case they returned.

"Well, there was one woman who came in with him a few times. She was about his age, pretty, and with shoulder length brown hair."

I smiled. "That's helpful. One other question since we're new in town."

"Yes?"

"There seems to be a big fuss regarding the town's fairgrounds. I heard some people want the city to take it over and turn it into a strip mall, while others are adamant that it remains in Hargrove's hands. Do you have any idea why people love it so much? It looks kind of run down."

"Tell me about it. I took my grandson there last year and it was showing a lot of wear. If there is some reason to keep it, no one told me about it."

"Thanks."

Viola looked over her shoulder. "Sorry. I have other customers. What can I get you all to eat?"

I didn't care what I ordered since everything on the menu looked appetizing. We'd just eaten several large meals in a row, so I went with a salad and the baked fish plate. I did not respond to Drake's raised brows at my restraint.

Once Viola took off to place our order, I leaned in closer. "Do any of you remember someone fitting that description at the party?"

"Not me, but why would Armand's possible mistress show up?" Andorra asked. "I would think Armand wouldn't want his wife to be more suspicious than she already was."

We all sat there for a moment. I couldn't think of any reason.

Jaxson sat up straighter. "What if she had no choice?"

"Meaning?" I asked.

"What if Trixie was the wife of an invited guest? This is a small town, remember?" Jaxson wiggled his brows.

That had a lot of potential. "We looked at the list of guest names, but I don't remember anyone named Trixie. When we get back, we'll ask your mom which of the wives it might be. Trixie could be a nickname."

Jaxson smiled. "Like pink lady?"

"Exactly." That was Jaxson's pet name for me.

Our meals arrived, and as I dug in, my thoughts bounced between infidelity and sentimentality. "Question for you all. Which is a stronger motive for murder? Jealousy or nostalgia?"

I had my opinion, but I wanted to hear their thoughts. The other three looked at each other for a moment.

Drake piped up. "Not being as experienced as you guys, I'd have to say jealousy. As for nostalgia, a person might fight to keep the fairgrounds, but I don't see killing over it."

"I have to agree," I said. "Does this mean we don't need to focus so much on the two women who want to keep the fairgrounds open any more? Mary Jo claimed it was part of Magnolia's history. While true, I don't see killing over it."

"We probably should lower their rankings," Jaxson suggested.

Since we didn't know Trixie's real name, we'd reached another dead end. After we finished our meal and left a nice tip for our gossipy Viola, we returned to Jaxson and Drake's parents' home.

When we walked in, Maddy and Eugene were chatting. They stopped and looked up. "Any luck with learning who Trixie is?" Maddy asked.

We shucked off our jackets and sat down. "Yes and no."

I detailed what Viola said, and then Jaxson asked to look at the guest list.

Maddy handed it to us. "None of the wives are named Trixie," she said.

"Could it be a name from high school? Most people have or are given nicknames," Jaxson said.

Drake looked over at Andorra. "We had one for Andorra."

Her eyes widened. “Don’t you dare.”

My memory snapped into place. “Olive Oil,” I blurted.

“I hated that name.” Andorra looked over at Jaxson’s parents. “It was stupid. I was really skinny, and the kids somehow knew about that super old cartoon, Popeye. His girlfriend, Olive Oil, was really thin.”

Drake squeezed her hand. “You’re perfect now.”

“Aw, thank you.” Andorra blew him a kiss.

Eugene picked up the paper. “That gives me an idea.” He scanned the list. “Often the nickname has a reason for existing. Bea Jones might be Trixie. Her real name is Beatrix, right?”

“Yes,” Maddy said.

“Trixie could be short for Beatrix.”

“That’s a good guess. Let’s keep her in mind. Does Bea have brown hair? And would you say she was pretty?”

Maddy looked over at her husband. “I would say she fits the bill.”

“She’s not a suspect, is she?” Andorra asked. “If she was having an affair with Armand, she might want to get rid of Lydia, not Armand.”

“That makes sense.” That seemed to be yet another dead end. I turned to Jaxson’s parents. “Did Wilson reveal any big secrets?”

“As a matter of fact, he might have,” Eugene said.

“Do tell.”

CHAPTER NINE

"I BELIEVE it was Genevieve who found out that high schoolers would often visit the fairgrounds at night. We can all guess what might be going on there." Eugene raised his brows. He looked so much like Jaxson when my fiancé did the same movement that my heart pinged.

"I'm following so far," I said.

"Wilson told us that Mary Jo Harper and Sharon Graeber were best buddies in high school."

"What does that have to do with anything, Dad?" Jaxson asked.

"Just saying, these two could be in cahoots."

I wasn't seeing it. "To kill Armand? Even you said his death wouldn't change the outcome of the vote."

"*I* know that, but maybe they didn't."

Before we could ask what other tidbit of gossip Wilson had imparted, Genevieve and Hugo appeared.

"Hey, guys, what did we miss?" she asked.

"I'm honestly not sure we've uncovered much." I told her about Viola's take on things. "It's possible that Bea Jones, Daniel Lee's wife, was having an affair with Armand."

She grinned. "Does that mean that Daniel Lee killed Armand?"

"Why? Do you think he killed the man who was trying to steal his wife?"

"It's possible."

"Okay, I'll put Daniel Lee's name down. The whole poison thing seems a bit off, but we can figure that out later. What else did you two learn?"

Genevieve checked with Hugo and then turned back to her captive audience. "Lydia was on the phone for a while with someone named Lizzy."

"Lizzy Davenport," Eugene said. "They are really good friends. Lizzy works as a receptionist at the courthouse."

"Was she at the party?" I asked.

"As a matter of fact she was."

My mind tried out a few scenarios, but I wanted to hear what else Genevieve had learned. "Go on."

"Hugo is better than I am at keeping out of a person's way when they are moving about, so he listened into most of the conversation. This Lizzy friend was telling Lydia that she needed to sell the house and move on, now that she has the means to do so."

"How did Lydia respond?" I asked.

Genevieve looked over at Hugo once more. "He said that Lydia agreed. I watched her the whole time. She was not all that upset that Armand was dead. In fact, the more they talked, the angrier Lydia became."

"Can we all conclude that Lydia Linfield won't be wearing black for long?" I asked.

"Why black?" Genevieve asked.

I forgot that our gargoyle shifter had only been in the human realm for a short time. I explained about the tradition of wearing black when a person was in mourning.

"Got it."

"If she had the means to move on, does that mean Lydia will receive insurance money?" Drake asked. "Or were they already well-off?"

"I don't think that she and Armand were swimming in money, but I could be wrong," Eugene said. "I'll see if I can find out. I have a friend in insurance."

"Great." I went over to the white board and listed a few more names. Their motive seemed obvious—that of jealousy. "I guess I need to add the supportive friend Lizzy, though I can't imagine someone killing her friend's husband just to take revenge on him for cheating on Lydia."

Maddy's face heated. "It might be that Lizzy wanted Lydia for herself."

Whoa. My mind hadn't gone in that direction. "Okay. I'll put down Lizzy's name then."

We decided on ranks for each of the suspects, but at this moment, I was more confused than ever. We had too many suspects, which seemed to be worse than having none at all.

Pete hopped forward. "I've been thinking."

"About what?" I asked.

"People tend to ignore us animals since we aren't human, but we see things."

I had no idea where he was going with this, but I liked it. "I imagine that's true."

"Maddy watches a lot of crime shows on television, and to be honest, they were the only things that kept me sane."

"Oh, Pete," Maddy said. "I am so sorry. If I had known, I could have done more for you."

He fluffed his feathers, which I guess was his way of shrugging. "What have you figured out, Pete?" I asked.

"Everything revolves around the fairgrounds. Don't you agree?"

"That or infidelity," I said. "At this point, I'm not sure if the murder was motivated by town politics or by personal need."

"If it has to do with the town wanting to use the

fairgrounds for its own personal gain, I'd like to check out the place—from above. Like a drone," Pete said.

From Pete's vocabulary, he had been watching a lot of crime shows. Maybe too many.

Jaxson glanced around. "Pete, what do you hope to find?" he asked.

"If I knew that, I wouldn't have to do a fly over, now would I?"

Zing. I think Pete had been hanging around Iggy too much. As interesting as it would be to see what he could notice, it would be best to let the Harrison's decide what to do.

"Pete, you've not been outside before, except in the car when we've taken you to the vet," Eugene said.

"Which is why I need to explore. I'm no ordinary bird. I can become invisible if need be."

"I had no idea." Eugene looked over at Maddy. "What do you think?"

"I don't know. Pete, we love you. If you were hurt or lost, I'd be devastated."

Hugo stepped forward. "He says he'll go with Pete," Genevieve said. "While Hugo can't fly, he can teleport. He'll keep your parrot safe."

Maddy blew out a breath. "If I'd been in a cage for twenty years, I'd want to explore too. But don't be gone long, okay?"

Pete practically jumped up and down. "Okay."

"Since it's dark, you won't be able to see much. How about you go tomorrow morning?" she suggested.

"I'm a bird. I can see at night, but I can go tomorrow if you'd feel better."

"I would. Thank you."

I looked over at Genevieve. "Does Hugo know where the fairgrounds are?"

"Yes, but in case he needs to call for help, I'll go too."

"They've been gone a long time," Maddy said as she picked up the empty platter that had held the scrambled eggs.

She really cared for Pete. "He'll be fine," I said, trying to assure her. "Hugo and Genevieve won't let anything happen to Pete."

"I hope so." She carried the dish into the kitchen.

Andorra and I jumped up to help Maddy clear the table. We placed our dirty dishes next to the sink.

"Maddy, if they are taking their time, maybe they found something," Andorra said.

"I know, but Pete has never left the house by himself before."

"He's with two very capable people," I said. That sounded better than saying two gargoyle shifters.

"Mom, come here," Jaxson called from the dining room.

From the sound of his voice, he was excited. The three of us rushed into the dining room, and who should be there but our three explorers.

Maddy rushed over to Pete and picked him up. "Are you okay?"

"Am I okay? I'm incredible. There is a whole world out there. It was amazing."

I was very happy he had a good time, but the real question was did he find anything? "Is there anything you want to tell us?"

He bobbed his head. "I can see into the ground, I think."

"What does that mean, Pete?" Jaxson asked.

Pete hopped onto the now cleared dining room table. "I flew over the fairgrounds, and at times, I could see stuff buried under the ground."

"Like what? Garbage or a lost item?" I asked.

"I don't know, but Hugo thinks that Ruby might be able to enhance my ability. Like what you and your other friend did for Iggy."

I looked over at Andorra. "What do you think?"

"We could ask Elizabeth to come here, but it will take her a few hours. If she comes, I'd have to go back to help cover her shift at the store."

"I can take you," Genevieve said.

"Wait!" Thankfully, she didn't whisk Andorra back

to Witch's Cove instantly. "Andorra, if we do this, we'll need the ingredients for the spell. If you could ask Bertha about it, that would be great. If she doesn't remember what we used, can you contact Levy? He provided me the spell the last time."

"Sure." I had her take down Levy's number just in case. Andorra pushed back her chair and stood. "Let me get my jacket and purse, okay?"

For once, Genevieve listened. I honestly wasn't that hopeful the spell would work, especially since Levy wasn't with us, but it was worth a try.

After Andorra gathered what she needed, Genevieve placed a hand on her shoulder, and they disappeared.

"Maybe I should have gone with her," Drake said.

"If all goes well, Elizabeth will return with Ruby in no time. Once we do the spell, Elizabeth can return home, and Andorra will be back," I said.

"I suppose I can always hitch a ride with Hugo if need be, though I've never teleported before," Drake said.

"It's a little creepy at first, but it's not painful or anything. One second you are here, and then the next you aren't."

"May I ask who Ruby is?" Maddy asked.

"Mom, Ruby is a cat, but she's also a familiar. She talks and is quite powerful," Jaxson said.

"You know I'm allergic to cats."

"I know, but Ruby might not be like other cats. But

go ahead and take your allergy meds. It's best to be safe," Jaxson said.

Maddy left, and the rest of us moved into the living room. Pete's insistence on needing more power seemed a bit contrived. It was almost as if he wanted to compete with Iggy, since my familiar had been given some super powers for a day.

"Pete, are you saying that you think you possess some kind of X-ray vision? Kind of like ground penetrating radar?" Assuming he knew what that was, though if he watched enough crime shows, he should.

"Maybe. At times, I could see solid objects under the dirt and at other times, I saw nothing. It's hard to explain. It was like my abilities came and went."

I wish I could tell if he was making this up or not. I suppose if Elizabeth and I did the spell, it wouldn't make things worse.

About thirty minutes later, Genevieve arrived with Elizabeth and Ruby in tow.

"Whoa. That was intense," Elizabeth said.

If this was her first time teleporting, it would be quite the experience.

Jaxson introduced her to his parents and Pete.

Ruby wiggled in Elizabeth's arm. "Let me meet the man of the hour."

Elizabeth set the cat down. She walked over to the parrot, jumped up onto the coffee table, and studied him. He flapped his wings, probably to show his dominance, but Ruby wasn't having anything to do with that. She swiped at him but didn't connect, which was most likely on purpose.

Elizabeth's brows pinched. "Ruby, behave, please. We are trying to solve a murder."

"Fine, but this bird needs to behave too."

Ouch. She was a sassy one.

"Do you have the ingredients for the spell?" I asked Elizabeth.

"I do." She slipped off her purse from her shoulder. "Where do you want to set up?"

"The dining room is good," Maddy said.

We all moved back in there and then set out the bowls, the candles, and the ingredients. When we did this with Iggy and Ruby last month, it took many, many tries to get it right. I explained to Pete that Ruby needed to be touching him in order for the power to be enhanced or transferred. I really didn't understand how it worked, other than it did.

"Fine, but be gentle," Pete told Ruby.

"Iggy wasn't so squeamish," she mumbled.

She was on a roll today. Clearly, she and Pete wouldn't become best friends anytime soon. Or maybe they would once Pete gained some powers.

"Fine, do your thing," Pete shot back.

Elizabeth and I went over the spell. "Ready?" I asked them.

They both nodded. Once Ruby pressed against Pete,

we lit the candles and said the spell. I truly believed that Ruby could provide Pete with some powers. The question was whether or not it was the power he needed in order to see what was in the ground.

I also didn't know how this was going to help us in anyway solve Armand Linfield's murder. I was doing it more as a way to make it up to him for being in a cage for twenty years. Pete deserved to have some fun.

Once we finished with the spell, Ruby stepped away. "I think Pete's good now."

"How can you tell?" I asked her.

"I just can. He can go outside and fly around to test it out if he wants."

That made sense. Without asking, Hugo picked up Pete and disappeared. I had no idea if they were going for a spin around the neighborhood or if they were heading back to the fairgrounds.

"Now what?" Maddy asked. "Did Ruby give Pete powers?"

"We'll see. Ruby was amazing the last time," I said.

The cat stretched her back. "You bet I was."

She certainly didn't lack self-confidence. I thought Pete and Hugo would return in a few minutes, but they didn't. "Genevieve, did they go to the fairgrounds?"

"Yes. They are there now. I should supervise." And poof.

"Why doesn't everyone go back into the living room

and wait for them to return while Elizabeth and I clean up the mess from the spell?"

As the group stood and left, Ruby jumped off the table. She actually waited for Iggy to climb down. I was surprised when the two of them headed off together. Their bond seemed to be strong after our last spell.

It was at least an hour before our surveyors returned, and when they did, Genevieve was grinning. "You will not believe what Pete found."

CHAPTER TEN

Genevieve was always a bit dramatic, but from the way Pete was flapping his wings, they must have hit pay dirt. “Well, someone needs to tell us.”

Genevieve nodded to Pete. He flew to the coffee table and landed. Clearly, he wanted everyone’s attention. “I saw a body.”

“A dead body?” Drake asked.

Pete faced Drake. “Most people in the ground are dead.”

Pete was developing quite the snarky personality.

“But this person was actually *in* the ground?” I asked.

“Yup. I could see right through the dirt. It was like the soil didn’t even exist. This spell is really cool. Most of the objects were small things, like rocks and probably coins and stuff, but...then I saw it.”

I was so thankful that Iggy wasn't this long winded. "Saw what?"

"The body! Or rather the remains of a body."

Whoa. I looked over at Genevieve. "Did you see anything?" I asked her.

"No, but we marked the spot if you want to dig it up."

I looked over at Jaxson. "We'd need a warrant for that, right?"

"Not if Jack Hargrove says it's okay to check it out." He faced his father. "What do you think? Telling Jane Waters that our parrot is magical and has X-ray vision will probably land one of us in the loony bin."

His father nodded. "No doubt. Jane doesn't cotton to such nonsense."

Once more I thanked our good stars for having Steve Rocker as our sheriff. He believed in magic—more or less. Of late, it had been more, especially since he'd seen a ghost and could now communicate with Iggy.

"Do you think Mr. Hargrove will be there now?" I asked.

"I'll check." That came from Genevieve who left a split second later. Hopefully, she remembered us mentioning that his trailer was at the back of the fair-grounds.

When she didn't return right away, I was tempted to ask Hugo to see what she was up to. If the owner spotted someone appearing out of nowhere, it might cause him to have a heart attack, and that was the last thing we wanted or needed.

Fifteen minutes later, Genevieve returned. "Oh, my. Mr. Hargrove is just a nice man."

I dreaded hearing what she'd done. "Why is that?"

"He gave me some tea, and then when I explained about having X-ray vision—yes, yes, I know I should have told him it was Pete, but come on. I don't think he would have believed that a bird can do that."

"Did he believe that *you* could see through things—like the ground?"

She shook her head. "No, but I flirted a bit and asked if I could dig up a tiny, tiny part of the property to make sure. I lied and told him that my great grandfather disappeared years and years ago, and that he was last seen at the fairgrounds."

I had to hand it to her. She was inventive. "Did he ask how long ago this relative had been missing?"

Her shoulders drooped as Genevieve's mouth twisted up. "I don't think he asked."

I suppose it didn't matter. "Did he agree to let you dig up your dead relative?"

"He sure did. He said he'll leave the gate unlocked for you."

"Dad, will there be any repercussions for you if we go out to the fairgrounds and check it out?" Jaxson said.

"Not directly, but what happens if Pete is right and there is a dead body?" Eugene asked.

Pete puffed out his chest. "I am right."

Maddy sat up straighter, her face twisted in worry. "Maybe you should let it go. Don't we have enough to worry about with Armand being dead? Why dig up a new body?"

She had a point. "I would agree except that I have this strange witchy feeling that this body is connected somehow to Armand's death."

Her brows rose. "Why would you think that?"

"Let's say that we had a kind of similar case exactly one year ago that involved finding a fifty-year-old body that tied the past with the present."

"I think Jaxson did mention something like that. The body was in the candy store."

"That's the one."

Jaxson looked over at Drake. "You up for a little digging?"

"Now?"

"Why not? If it turns out to be nothing, it will help burn off those Christmas calories."

He smiled. "Count me in. Dad, do you have a shovel?"

"Only one. You'll have to stop at the hardware store and get another one."

Jaxson slapped his thighs. "Who wants to come?"

Andorra raised her hand. "Me."

Genevieve had already *escorted* Elizabeth and Ruby back to Witch's Cove and had returned with Andorra. I hoped she wasn't too tired to do this as my curiosity wouldn't let me leave it alone.

"Me, too, but it's too cold for Iggy."

"Thanks, leave me here," he huffed.

Maddy leaned over. "Iggy if you stay here, I'll fix you a pile of lettuce, and I have some flowers that I'd purchased for the Christmas party that you can have. I don't want to throw them out."

He spun around twice. "Yippee. I get my own feast."

I chuckled. Iggy did love his flowers.

"Hugo and I have to show you all where the body is located," Genevieve said.

"I can help too," Pete said.

I suppose he could keep a look out for us. "Sure."

Maddy stood. "I'll make a couple of thermoses of hot chocolate since it may take you a few hours. It can get cold out there if the sun's not out. I'll also toss in a few sandwiches if you get hungry."

She was so sweet. "Thanks."

Once we changed our clothes for the adventure, I made sure to take some extra warm clothes should it turn too cold for my thin Florida blood. By the time we were set, Maddy had our refreshments all packed.

"Good luck," Eugene said. "If you find anything, call Jane. Otherwise, my tenure at the courthouse might be in jeopardy."

"Sure, Dad," Jaxson said.

If we located a body, I don't know what reason we could tell the sheriff that she'd believe as to why we were digging in the fairgrounds in the first place. She wouldn't believe we had a parrot who possessed ground penetrating radar vision. If there was a test we could do to convince her that magic existed, it would help. We couldn't chance Genevieve or Hugo teleporting Jane away from Magnolia. Who knew how freaked out she'd become?

Genevieve, Hugo, and Pete said they would meet us at the fairgrounds since we needed to stop at the hardware store first. Once inside, the men picked up some gloves, an extra shovel, and some garbage bags. Jaxson's dad had tossed a few folding chairs, two blankets, and some flashlights in the back of Jaxson's truck so that Andorra and I could sit and watch. Yes, we could dig, but the men seemed willing to do the work.

Once we arrived, our two gargoyles and parrot showed us where they'd marked this grave. As we trudged to the far ends of the fairgrounds, I was beginning to see the folly of this. Even if Pete was right, did we really need the hassle of one more body?

Sheriff Waters might accuse Drake or Jaxson of having something to do with the death. How else would they know where to dig?

The problem was that we all stood for justice, which meant there was no way I was going to talk Jaxson out of doing this. And if we ignored Pete, he'd never be the same. Let's hope the spell Elizabeth and I put on him hadn't made him delusional.

True to Genevieve's word, they'd stuck sticks in the ground, as well as circled the area with rocks. It was rather clever, especially since the possible gravesite was in a secluded wooded area.

We set up our chairs, poured some hot chocolate, and sat back to watch the Harrison boys do some back work.

Pete and Genevieve patiently waited nearby for their next assignment. I had no idea where Hugo was. I suspected he was on guard duty somewhere.

After watching the men slave for over thirty minutes, Pete flapped his way over to the edge of the grave. "Take it easy. You're getting close."

Jaxson stopped. "How close? Three inches or a foot?"

Pete hopped down into the hole. From where I was sitting, I couldn't see what was going on, but I figured he was using his super power to locate the body. We had some flashlights pointing into the hole, though I didn't know if he needed light.

"Five inches," Pete announced with some authority.

Jaxson and Drake slowed down their digging speed. When a clink sounded, both men stopped.

"I hit something," Drake said.

Together, they squatted down and dug with their hands.

"Can one of you ladies shine the light down here?" Jaxson said.

The three of us each grabbed one of the lights and then shined them down into the hole. It didn't take long before Drake lifted up what was surely a bone.

"Well, I'll be," he said.

Pete flew up the surface. "Told you I'm good."

"You are, Pete." I knew how much he probably needed the affirmation. "Shouldn't one of us call the sheriff?" I asked.

"Drake, you should. Jane doesn't like me."

Both men climbed out of the hole and sat on the edge, their faces covered in sweat and dirt, and their shirts and jeans filthy.

"What will you tell her?" I asked. "She's going to ask why we were digging in this spot."

"She will assume we were trying to move the body," Jaxson said.

"Let's tell her the truth," Drake suggested. "She won't believe us, but the fact we called her before digging up more of the remains should prove to her that we are innocent."

I snapped my fingers. "I think I might know how we can prove to her that we didn't kill anyone and that we are trying to be good citizens." Okay, that might be a stretch.

"How?" Jaxson asked.

I turned to Pete. "Can you see through my purse and tell me what is inside?"

He waddled over to it and stood in front. "You have a brush, a wallet, and...what is that? A power bar?"

I always had a snack handy. "You are truly amazing. How about if Pete tells the sheriff what's in her purse?"

"Jane Waters would never carry a purse," Jaxson said.

"There has to be something in her pockets—a phone, a driver's license, or keys to her vehicle."

"Give it a try," Jaxson said.

Drake called the station and stated that he found the remains of a body in the fairgrounds. He did not say that he and Jaxson had dug a big hole to locate the body. That had been smart.

"How about Andorra and I head back to the parking lot and meet the sheriff? We'll show her where you are," I suggested.

Genevieve smiled. "I could always teleport her here. Then she'd have to believe in magic."

"That might cause more problems. Let's keep it as simple as possible."

"Fine. Whatever."

I'm sorry Genevieve was disappointed that she couldn't show off her skills, but it couldn't be helped. We needed the sheriff to trust us.

Andorra and I headed out to the fairgrounds' entrance to wait for Jane Waters. I knew she would ask us what happened, but Drake was right. We had to tell her the truth.

When the sirens neared, we hoofed it. We made it to the parking lot just as the three squad cars came to a halt. I was surprised that a town the size of Magnolia owned three cars, but I was comparing it to the size of the Witch's Cove fleet.

The sheriff stepped out of her vehicle, along with one of the deputies who'd been at the house. The other men I didn't recognize.

"Sheriff." I held out my hand and introduced myself and Andorra again, in case she forgot.

"I remember you two. So where is this body you found?"

Right to the point. I wouldn't expect any less from her. "It's in the woods on the far side of the fairgrounds."

She motioned that everyone follow. When one of the men stepped out of the car, I recognized him as the medical examiner. I probably should have said he wouldn't be needed. A forensic anthropologist would be a better bet.

"Glinda, how did you and the others find this body if it's in the woods?"

I inhaled. Not that I'd practiced my speech, but once I decided to tell the truth, my anxiety level reduced. "You won't believe me if I tell you."

"Try me."

"We found out that the Harrison's pet parrot they've had for twenty years possesses magic."

While she probably tried to contain it, a small laugh escaped. "Magic doesn't exist."

"But it does. I'm a witch."

"Fine. Tell me, how did this magical parrot find a dead body?"

Here goes. "My friend and I put a spell on Pete that enhances his X-ray vision ability, at least for a few hours." I kept going so she wouldn't tell me I was crazy. "He flew over the fairgrounds, looking for something, because the facts of the Armand Linfield case weren't adding up. We all were convinced that his murder had something to do with the fairgrounds—or maybe it was a result of his infidelity." I lifted a hand. "We thought we'd try the fairground angle first."

"I will admit that Mr. Linfield was an advocate for having the city put a strip mall here. Others opposed him."

"That's my main issue. *Why* oppose him? The place is a mess. Even the owner isn't sure he'll be opening again. If Mr. Hargrove were to dismantle the fair, is it fair—no pun intended—to make him sell his land—land he intends to give to his grandson?"

The sheriff actually seemed to be fighting a smile. "A born politician I see. Did you find out this from Jack Hargrove?"

"Yes."

She didn't say anything for a moment. "Do you know what obstruction of justice is?"

"Of course, but talking to a fairground owner isn't against the law."

"Maybe not technically," Jane Waters said, "but you are getting in my way. I'm trying to solve a murder—or two murders maybe."

What? I was never in her way. "Are you going to arrest us? We didn't break any law." Or at least I don't think we did.

"Not yet."

The flashlights were pointing to the location of the grave, and she picked up the pace. When we reached the gravesite, the men hadn't removed any more of the body, even though they had dug down several feet to expose a bone or two.

When we arrived, Pete pranced up to Sheriff Waters and looked up at her. She stilled. "Did you really find this body using magic?" she asked our feathered friend.

From her tone, it was clear she didn't believe that for one minute—or at least most of her didn't believe it. At least she was willing to humor us and Pete.

Pete nodded his head.

The sheriff stilled and then faced me. "Did he understand me?"

"Pete understands everything," I announced.

"If I tell him to sit on my deputy's shoulder, he'll do it?"

I wasn't sure how cooperative Pete would be, but if it was a chance to show off, he just might. "Ask him."

"Pete, can you—" She didn't have to finish her sentence since Pete had already heard what she told me.

To my delight, he flew straight to the deputy who naturally put up his arms in a defensive pose. That didn't deter Pete, however. He landed on the deputy's head to avoid the man's waving hands that were moving every which way.

"I hope she's happy now?" Pete said.

Too bad she couldn't hear him.

"Thank you, Pete. You can get down," Jane said.

He did.

The sheriff pressed her lips together as if she was trying to gain some composure. "Let's see this body of yours."

CHAPTER ELEVEN

While at the grave, leaves rustled behind us, and I turned around. To my surprise, it was Hugo carrying none other than Iggy. I rushed up to them. "What is Iggy doing here?" I managed to keep my voice low.

No, I couldn't hear Hugo's answer, but Iggy could translate. "He thought that if we need to give the sheriff a demonstration of magic that I could do my number trick."

"We could, but if we really want to show her magic, I could have Hugo and Genevieve teleport the sheriff somewhere." I wouldn't though. Since Hugo seemed to take all comments as commands, I held up my hand. "But don't even think about it, Hugo. That would be kidnapping an officer of the law. We are already on very shaky ground here—legally, that is. Jaxson doesn't need any trouble. Do you hear?"

Hugo nodded and then looked down. I probably shouldn't have used my teacher voice, but I kept forgetting that Hugo wasn't like Genevieve who wasn't a great listener.

I lifted Iggy from Hugo's arms and returned to the group. Hugo followed behind. The sheriff was standing over the hole as her deputies were grabbing the shovels and digging.

"Jaxson and Drake, may I have a word with you two?" the sheriff asked.

"Sure," they said in unison.

"Can you tell me how you stumbled upon the grave?"

Drake told her what happened—from how Iggy learned that Pete could talk to how Elizabeth and I put a spell on him that allowed him to better see things underground. "He can probably give you a demonstration if you'd like."

I like that our stories—however outrageous they may sound to her—matched.

Pete, who'd been listening to the conversation, hopped up to the sheriff and studied her for a moment. "You have a wallet in your left pocket, a cell phone with a black case in your top pocket, and a key ring with four keys in your back pocket." Pete looked up at us. "She has on gray underwear, but I don't think you should tell her that. She'll arrest me for being inappropriate."

I swallowed a laugh. I figured Jaxson could tell her what Pete said, which he did.

Jane Waters emptied her pockets. It didn't surprise me that she had a wallet, a phone with a black case, and a keychain with four keys. "How did you know?" She looked around at us. "I know the wallet and the phone bulge in my pockets, but how did you know about the keys?"

"Pete told us," Jaxson said. "Like we mentioned. He talks, and he has X-ray vision."

She whistled. "How again did you know to send Pete out on this mission?"

Once more I went through my logic about how I saw no reason why Mary Jo Harper and Sharon Graeber would be so adamant about making sure that the strip mall wasn't built here, unless there was something they did not want unearthed.

"My dad learned from our neighbor that Mary Jo and Sharon were best buds in high school," Jaxson told her.

"I learned that high school kids came here a lot," Genevieve added.

The sheriff faced her and pulled out a pad to write down her name. "Who are you again?"

"Hugo and I work at the Hex and Bones Apothecary store back in Witch's Cove. Andorra's grandmother is the owner."

That lacked some accuracy, but it would do in a pinch.

The deputy stood and motioned the sheriff over. "We have the skull and part of the body so far," he announced in a voice loud enough for us to hear.

Naturally, we had to check it out. To my surprise, the skeleton had on some clothes, or I should have said he or she had on deteriorated strips of fabric across some bones.

"Any idea how long the body has been here?" the sheriff asked.

"That's hard to say. I can tell you it's a male in his early twenties," the medical examiner told her. "From the decay, he's been here a long time. We'll need to ask Dr. Andrews to do the investigation. I'm good when there is skin and organs. Forensic anthropology isn't my forte."

She tapped her notepad against hers lips, clearly debating what to do next. "It's late, but I'll give him a call tomorrow morning. Let's hope Danny is available. In the meantime, let's cover up the grave. We don't need animals messing with the site."

Danny? She must know the doctor well.

One of the deputies offered to contact the owner to see what he knew about the body. If Jack Hargrove had anything to do with the man's death, I doubt he'd say anything. On the other hand, he might say it was a relative of Genevieve's. Oh, boy. That would be hard to explain.

Jane faced us all. "Thank you all for sending your magical bird to find this grave but don't leave town. I may have more questions."

I bet she would.

"No problem," Jaxson said.

Drake stiffened. He couldn't stay indefinitely, and I didn't want to be here for weeks either. When she nodded in the direction of the parking lot, we took the hint. After gathering our equipment, we left. Part way to the parking lot, our two gargoyle shifters disappeared. Genevieve had Pete with her, but I had Iggy. Good thing, too, since he tended to convince others to do his bidding, and we didn't need Genevieve, Pete, or Hugo following Iggy's advice.

We piled into our cars and took off before any of the officers returned to the lot. "That went about as well as we could hope," Jaxson said.

"Because the sheriff didn't arrest you on the spot?" I asked.

"Yup."

"I have to say, your sheriff took things pretty well. Pete did a good job of convincing her magic was involved," I said.

"We'll see what she comes back with in a few days. I'm not convinced she really believed us. Heck, I'm not sure I would."

"True." For the remainder of the short ride home, I wanted to figure out what we could do to help speed things along. I twisted toward the back seat. "What do you all think about having Genevieve and Hugo listen in on what the sheriff is doing? Our two shifters don't seem to have a problem standing watch twenty-four seven."

"That sounds good. I bet Genevieve would be happy to be involved," Andorra said.

"I'll play the devil's advocate," Jaxson said. "What if Genevieve and Hugo learn something important? We then use that information to find proof that a particular person killed that poor man in the ground. How would you explain to Jane where we procured the information?"

Once more, he was a spoilsport. "Can we worry about that later? If we learn who the dead man is, by the time we figure out who killed him, Jane might have divulged his identity." I knew that was very convoluted logic.

"We'll see." Jaxson pulled into his parents' driveway. "Leave everything but the thermoses and the food in the truck. I'll take care of it in the morning."

We piled out. As soon as we entered the house, Drake called out to his parents, "We're home."

Maddy came out of the kitchen. "What did you find?"

"Mom, let us clean up, and then we'll tell you about the body we found."

"A body? Do you know who it was?" she asked.

Drake chuckled. "It was a skeleton, so no."

"Okay. Even though it's late, let me fix you all something to eat. I bet you boys are hungry."

"You have no idea. We didn't get a chance to eat the sandwiches you made." Jaxson glanced over at us girls.

I held up my palms, refusing to admit guilt.

Pete was in his cage. "I see Genevieve and Hugo returned with Pete, but where are they?" I asked no one in particular.

"They disappeared," Maddy said as if it was now a commonplacc occurrence.

That was so typical of them. I could guess what they were doing—staying close to the sheriff. We entered our rooms and took turns showering. Naturally, the men finished before we did.

When I entered the living room, I went up to Pete. "Where are your two cohorts?"

"Those two meanies?"

I huffed out a laugh. "Why would you say that?"

"I can cloak myself, so there is no reason why they couldn't have taken me with them. I didn't want to stay all night at the fairgrounds, but I could have kept Genevieve company at the sheriff's office."

Good information. "I bet if she learns anything

she'll come back and tell us. Maybe she'll take you on her next visit."

"Maybe."

Jaxson came over. "Mom set out some food for us in the kitchen. Come on."

I went with him. "Pete said that Genevieve and Hugo are scoping things out."

"Why am I not surprised?" Jaxson said.

Andorra and Drake were at the kitchen counter eating. We pulled up the remaining two seats and joined them.

"It could be days, bro, before that forensic guy gets down here, and then who knows how long it will take to identify the body. Does Sheriff Waters really expect us to stay here?" Drake asked.

"You could ask Genevieve to teleport you two back to Witch's Cove. If the sheriff needs to speak with you, she could call you," I suggested.

"That's not a bad idea. Where are those two anyway?" he asked.

I told them what Pete said.

"I wonder if they will ever stop going off on their own," Drake said.

"I doubt it."

I grabbed a sandwich and a drink. "Do you think the sheriff knows about genetic phenotyping?"

"What's that?" Jaxson asked.

I was kind of a science nut, so he shouldn't have

sounded surprised that I knew something he didn't. "I was doing some research a few months back and learned that we now have the technology to extract DNA from a dead body, even if it's from a skeleton. It almost doesn't matter the age. There is software that can process this DNA and then print out a picture of what the person might have looked like. Mind you, it's not perfect, but it's pretty accurate, or so they say."

"Wow. I've not heard of that," Drake said.

"I think it's been around for a bit, but like I mentioned, I just learned about it. We need to tell Steve about it when we return home," I said.

"Do you think Magnolia has such capabilities?" Jaxson asked. "This is not exactly a super technological town. And neither is Witch's Cove for that matter. That kind of equipment sounds really expensive."

"True, but there are a lot of big cities nearby that I bet have the capability," I said.

"Good point."

I yawned. It had been a long day. "Let's hope Genevieve comes back sometime tomorrow and fills us in."

"Let's hope."

It wasn't until close to dinnertime the next day that both Genevieve and Hugo returned. Considering the smile on her face, she had news.

"What did you learn?" Andorra asked.

"You better all sit down."

Our gargoyle was often a bit too dramatic, but if we wanted to find out what she knew, we had to play along. "Tell us," I said.

"Sheriff Jane is a hard worker. As soon as she returned to the office last night, she called some guy." Genevieve looked over at Hugo and then back at us. "Hugo listened in. I'm not sure Hugo understood everything, but according to him, Jane likes this guy, because she called him Danny."

Jaxson looked over at his mother. "Mom, is Jane dating anyone?"

"How would I know?"

I guess it didn't matter. "Go on."

"This person is a specialist in bones. She asked if he could take a look at the corpse. He said he'd get there the next day—which is today."

"That sounds hopeful that we'll get some answers soon then. What about the gravesite? Were they digging up the body when you last checked?"

Hugo nodded.

"I trust the bone guy was there to help the men know what to do?" Drake asked.

Once more, Hugo nodded.

"I wonder how long it will take them to finish, extract the DNA, and process it?" I asked.

"I bet it will take days or maybe even weeks. It's not like those television shows where they process DNA in fifteen minutes," Drake said. "Which is a long winded way of saying that I need to get back to the store. If the sheriff needs to ask me questions, have her call me."

"You take off, bro. I can answer any questions she might have," Jaxson said.

"Are you going back, too, Andorra?" I asked.

"I need to." She turned to Genevieve. "Do you mind staying a little longer and do some more spying?"

"Are you kidding? Of course. But first I have to teleport you two back to Witch's Cove. That will only take a few seconds, though."

"Great. We'll pack up."

While spying was illegal, I really wanted to hear what Genevieve discovered. If Jane questioned us, we had to act as if we knew nothing.

"Dad, did you ever hear about this murder that we think happened a long time ago?" Jaxson asked.

"No. We haven't lived in Magnolia that long, and the topic was never discussed, as far as I recall. Someone must have missed the poor guy, assuming he was a local."

"If he was buried, then I bet someone killed him," I tossed out.

"Most likely," Jaxson said. "Glinda, tomorrow, you

and I can go to the library and look through some old newspapers. I doubt Jane will have an identity before then."

"I can't remember, but did the medical examiner have a guess as to when he died?" I asked. "Or did he just know the man's age?"

"I know," Genevieve said.

"Oh, yeah? When?"

"I heard Jane talk to the forensic guy. He said the body had been in the ground about forty years. And the dead guy had a cracked skull."

"What? You're only now telling us about the cracked skull?"

She shrugged. "I forgot."

Sheesh. "Sounds like someone hit him on the head, and the blow killed him."

"Genevieve, keep up the good work," Jaxson said. "That's very valuable information."

I shouldn't have jumped down her throat for not presenting the information in order. "Yes, you did great."

Genevieve stood. "We'll get back to work then."

"Isn't the sheriff's office closed?" I asked.

"Probably, but there should be files from forty years ago, right?"

That was going too far. "You can't snoop like that."

She grinned. "I know, but I'm going to anyway, just as soon as I chauffeur Drake and Andorra home."

CHAPTER TWELVE

I SCOOTED my library chair closer to the table and then pulled my sweater tighter around my shoulders. The city certainly wasn't spending much money on heating this place. "I know I said it was wrong for Genevieve to snoop, but I'm glad she is. My eyes are blurring just looking through all of these newspaper articles. Whoever this dead guy is, it doesn't seem as if anyone missed him."

Jaxson had worked his magic on the computer regarding unsolved crimes and missing persons, but nothing showed up.

"He could have been passing through town, or he could have been a vagrant, which means no one might have reported his disappearance," Jaxson said.

"I get it. If he isn't local, any information regarding him might be in his hometown newspaper."

"If he died forty years ago, I doubt anyone is still searching for him, though," Jaxson said.

"Sad, but true. I just hope he was doing something that warranted a hit on the head. I hate to think he was an innocent victim."

Jaxson leaned back in his chair. "You've mentioned a few times that there might be a connection between this man's death and the death of Armand. Why is that again?"

"I don't have any hard facts. It's more of a feeling."

"But you told the sheriff that Armand's death probably revolved around the fairgrounds, right?" he asked.

"Yes. I figured why would someone fight so hard to keep this fair going?"

Jaxson's eyes widened. "Because this person doesn't want anyone to find a buried body." He smiled. "Smart."

"Like I said, it's my gut telling me something."

"We've trusted your gut before. We should go back to the house and look at the white board again. Maybe we can find a connection between this man and someone, say, who is about sixty years old," Jaxson said.

"Do you also think it's possible that someone killed this guy forty years ago, and then to make certain no development company came in and uncovered the body, he killed Armand?"

"I do. Like you always say, we need to keep an open mind about these things." Jaxson wiggled his brows.

"It's as good a theory as any." I logged out of the

computer I'd been staring at for over an hour. "I'm ready to head out anyway. Do you think your mom has any leftover sandwiches? All this investigation has given me an appetite."

Jaxson grinned. "That's my girl—and yes, Mom always has food when we are home."

When we arrived back at the house, it was kind of odd not to have Andorra or Drake there, but I understood they needed to return to work.

Surprisingly, Genevieve was sitting in the living room with Maddy and Eugene. However, Hugo was not there—at least not in his visible form.

"I didn't expect to find you here. Do you have news?" I asked her.

She lifted a piece of paper from her lap and handed it to me. It was an image of a young man. "Your sheriff seems to be able to convince everyone to do her bidding. I was impressed," she said.

Really? "I take that to mean the forensic anthropologist managed to extract some DNA from the skeleton?"

"Yes," she said. "And someone in another town ran that software stuff you were talking about."

"Very cool." I didn't want to ask how she snagged a copy of his image.

"Does he look familiar?" she asked.

"Not only am I not from here, I wasn't around forty years ago. So, no, I have no idea who he is." I handed the paper to Jaxson in case he'd seen the man's face during his library search, but he shook his head. "Dad, Mom, you don't know who he is, do you?"

"How could we? We were living in Witch's Cove when this man died—or at least I was. Your mom hadn't moved there yet."

"It was a stab in the dark," Jaxson said.

That stunk. "I wonder how Jane was able to get some lab to process the DNA so fast?" I looked around. "And don't you find it odd that the sheriff would ask to put a rush on an old case?"

"Maybe Jane, too, thinks this death relates to Armand's murder," Maddy said.

"Genevieve," Eugene said. "You spoke to someone who said that Mary Jo and Sharon were friends in high school, right?"

"Yes."

He picked up his coffee and took a sip. "I'm betting Jane is aware of that and will question them. They are both in their late fifties. Genevieve, maybe you could do a little more snooping to see if the sheriff learns anything new."

"Sure, but do you know where these women live in case the sheriff is with them now?"

He smiled. "I sure do. Come into my office, and I'll show you on the map."

Five minutes later, Eugene emerged—alone. "Mission accomplished. Genevieve will check out both women as well as the sheriff."

"It's a place to start," I said.

Pete squawked. "What can I do?"

Jaxson walked over to Pete's cage and let the poor thing out. He'd told us he didn't mind being in there, but that he liked to have the freedom to roam now and again. I hope that didn't mean he wanted to explore outside.

"I wish I knew, Pete. Right now, we have to wait for this dead man you found to be identified," Jaxson said.

While it seemed like hours had passed, it was no more than forty-five minutes before Genevieve returned. "I know what killed Armand." She grinned. "Okay, I'll tell you since I know you'll just ask. He was injected with poison."

Jaxson pumped a fist. "That means it wasn't my mother's cookie that did him in."

"Nope. The medical examiner guy found a needle mark on his shoulder."

I whistled. "That must have been some fast acting stuff. Did she say what the poison was?"

"The forensic guy gave the sheriff a name, but I can't remember that science stuff. All I remember is that he said it was some kind of liquid pesticide."

Eugene spoke up. "And we know who works at a pesticide company."

"Sid Harper," I shot back.

"Yup."

In the past, I would jump to conclusions, but I was more cautious now. "That's not proof he injected Armand, though."

"No," Eugene said. "But if he wanted to help his wife keep the fairgrounds, he might have."

"Being a nice guy and resorting to murder doesn't seem to go together, but I could be wrong. We'll definitely keep him in the running, though," I said.

"Dad, did you ever find out whether there was a life insurance policy on Armand?" Jaxson asked.

"No. It slipped my mind." He stood. "I'll make a few calls now."

Maddy went to fix everyone a snack just as Iggy crawled over to me. "Maybe this Sid guy killed the man in the park, and his wife is trying to protect him by not having that building put up."

I looked over at Jaxson. "That has potential."

"Sid is almost sixty. The timing works. I wonder if he knows who this person is, though if he is the murderer, he won't admit to recognizing him," Jaxson said.

"You can bet Jane will show this photo to everyone who was at the party—or at least to everyone over fifty," I added.

Jaxson nodded. "Jane will probably come here to show Mom and Dad the picture unless she remembers they didn't grow up here." He reached over and snatched the photo off the table. "I don't think it would be good if she saw that we already had this."

I huffed out a laugh. "You got that right."

Hugo appeared in front of us. He smiled and picked up Iggy.

"What did you learn?" Iggy asked.

My familiar said nothing for a few moments, implying Hugo was telling him a lot. Hugo then placed Iggy on the table, I guess to make it easier for him to tell us.

"Yes?" I asked.

"Hugo has been everywhere. But the big takeaway is that the bone doctor man found some skin under the man's nails."

"He had nails after all this time?"

"I'm just the messenger here. I never went to school, so I'm a little limited with this science stuff." Iggy lifted his head as if to challenge me.

"I used to be a teacher, remember? I'd be happy to teach you arithmetic, algebra, and maybe some basic biology, chemistry, and physics, if you want. Just let me know."

Iggy looked up at Hugo and then faced us. "I'll get back to you on that."

I figured. "Were they able to find out who's skin was under the dead man's nails?"

"No, because they couldn't find a match in their computers."

"The skin implies the man fought with his assailant," I said. "He must have scratched the person pretty good if there was a fair amount of cells." At least I thought that was how it worked.

"Yes, but the big question is whose is it?" Jaxson asked.

Maddy came out with some drinks. "Oh, Hugo. I didn't know you were here. Would you like something to drink?"

He smiled briefly and shook his head. I thought we'd mentioned he didn't need to eat or sleep—a benefit of being a gargoyle shifter.

She set our drinks on the coffee table. "I'll be right back with something for you, Iggy."

When she disappeared into the back, Iggy turned to Jaxson. "I really like your mom. She's always concerned about me." He spun to face me and puffed out his chest.

"Are you implying I don't make you my number one priority?" I couldn't help but raise my brows.

"Just saying."

I refused to be baited by my familiar.

Eugene came out of the office with a satisfied look on his face. "It took some doing, but I found out that Lydia Linfield took out a million dollar life insurance policy on her husband three months ago."

I whistled. "That's a lot of money—and it was recent, too. Did the agent say why?"

"Yes. Lydia claimed that Armand had received a few

threatening phone calls about the fairgrounds' proposal, and she was worried someone might act on that threat."

Jaxson sipped his coffee. "I wonder if Daniel Lee received those calls, too. Because if he did, then it would make sense that Lydia would want to be covered financially if anything happened to her husband."

"I can see where this day is going to be spent." His father turned around and headed back into his office.

"I bet he's going to see if either Armand or Daniel Lee reported these threatening calls," Jaxson said.

"Would you?"

"Report a call?" I nodded. "I guess it depends on whether the person told me to stop doing something specific. If he said he'd harm you if I didn't stop or if I called the police, then I would stop, and I wouldn't tell the cops."

That was so sweet of him. "I bet City Councilmembers get a lot of calls regarding their stance on topics. After a while, they might just ignore the threats," I said.

"Maybe."

Eugene came out of his office a few minutes later. "I spoke with Daniel Lee. He said he received some calls from concerned constituents who didn't want a strip mall, but it was nothing threatening."

"I guess we'll put Lydia a little higher on the list then," I announced.

"Dad, when you were on the City Council, did you receive threating phone calls?"

"Threatening? No. Just irate ones."

Maddy came out and sat down. "Figure out who killed Armand yet?"

"Not quite, Mom."

No sooner had Maddy joined us when a knock sounded on the door. For some reason, Hugo disappeared.

Eugene answered the door and then led Jane Waters inside. There were dark circles under her eyes, probably from lack of sleep.

"I have some questions for you—or rather for Maddy and Eugene."

I could guess what this was about.

"Have a seat, sheriff," Eugene said.

She handed them the image of the dead man and explained how it was procured. "Do you recognize him? He would have been here forty years ago."

To Eugene's credit, he studied the picture and acted as if it was the first time he'd seen it. "No, sorry. We weren't in the area at the time. In fact, Maddy and I hadn't even met yet."

Eugene looked over at his wife, smiled, and squeezed her hand. Aww. I hoped Jaxson and I were like that in forty years.

"Was he from around here?" Maddy asked.

"That we don't know. I've emailed the image to all of the nearby towns. I'm hoping that once we get a name,

I can run him through the criminal database, but he might have been an innocent passerby."

"Sheriff, something has been bugging me." I couldn't help myself. When something didn't fit, I had to speak up.

"What is that?" The sheriff didn't sound all that thrilled with me butting in.

"Do you often find victims of a homicide buried?"

"What do you mean?" she asked.

"This guy was at the fairgrounds, but I'd like to know why was he there? He could have been up to no good, or perhaps he was meeting someone there. But let's say a person came up behind him and attacked him. Wouldn't the killer take what he wanted and run? Who bothers to locate a shovel and bury him?"

"Glinda is right," Jaxson said. "It took Drake and me a long time to dig as far as we did. Wouldn't this attacker want to get away as quickly as possible? And if he dug a grave, it probably was at night."

"You think the killer might have known the victim and planned to kill him?" Jane asked.

"That hadn't occurred to me, but it's possible," I said.

"How did you know he had a contusion on the back of his skull?" Her gaze practically went right through me.

Whoops. "I just said he came up from behind him

and attacked him. Is that how he died? Someone smashed him in the head?"

"Possibly."

Why was she still looking at me? "You don't think we had anything to do with his death, do you?"

"No. The man was killed before you were born."

Good thing, too.

"Do we know what the man was bludgeoned with, Jane?" Eugene asked.

"It appeared to have an uneven surface."

"So not a shovel," I threw out.

"Probably not."

That sounded like the crime might not have been premeditated. "A rock, perhaps?"

"Perhaps." Jane's cell rang. "Excuse me." She checked the caller ID. "It's the deputy." She stood. "Sorry to have bothered you folks."

Eugene escorted her out. As soon as her car pulled out of the driveway, Hugo reappeared.

Iggy spun around. "Where did you go?" He bobbed his head at Hugo and then turned back to us. "Hugo needs help with his computer skills."

"Why is that?" I wasn't surprised our gargoyle shifter wasn't an accomplished computer guru since he'd spent most of his life as a statue.

"He couldn't find the registered complaints for the last six months at the sheriff's department."

That was smart of him to look. "Thanks for trying,

Hugo," I said. "I'm sure Jane will figure out that Lydia might have wanted to do her husband in, unless Armand actually registered the threatening calls with the sheriff's department."

"What's our next step?" Jaxson asked.

Before I could even think of something, Genevieve appeared. Once more she was smiling, which was always a good sign. "We got a hit off the photo," she answered.

A hit? She was improving rapidly with our slang. "Who was it?"

Genevieve blew out a breath. "I hope I remember everything the deputy said. The victim's name was Joey Franklin, and he lived in Citrus something."

"Citrus Park?" Maddy asked.

"Yeah. That's it. The call just came into the sheriff's office."

"That's what the deputy must have been calling Jane about," I said. "Go on."

"Turns out the guy had a record."

"For what?" Jaxson asked.

She rolled her eyes. "I can't remember exactly, but it was for something bad. I think assault."

"If this guy was looking for trouble, why go to the fairgrounds? Was he there to abduct someone? Or rob them?" I asked. "Or was he lured there by the killer?"

"Remember that Joey had a record," Jaxson said. "I'd go with the first scenario."

"Or, Joey could have been framed for a crime, and

the killer claimed to have information on his case," I said.

Jaxson held up a hand. "You are absolutely right. We can't know for sure if Joey was the good guy here or the bad guy. All we know is that Joey and the killer fought, as evidenced by the skin cells under his nails."

"I know what happened!" Iggy said. "Or I can guess."

This ought to be good. "What's that?"

CHAPTER THIRTEEN

"The dead man scratched someone, right?" Iggy asked.

"If he had something under his fingernails, then yes," I said.

"Let's say Hugo is the victim. I know that is ridiculous since Hugo would just disappear, but pretend he's an ordinary human." Iggy really seemed to be excited about his theory.

"I follow you so far," I said.

"Maybe this Joey Franklin thug knocks Hugo down and then stands over him. He might be kicking the—"

I held up a hand. "We don't need all of the details. Hugo, here, is not in a good spot—we get it. Go on."

He turned to Hugo. "Can you get on the ground for me?"

Hugo might have asked why, but we couldn't hear if he did.

Iggy hopped down next to his prone friend. "So, I'm thinking that maybe Hugo grabs the bad guy's leg and knocks Joey to the ground. They fight." To simulate what was happening, Iggy jumped onto Hugo's chest, and Hugo picks up Iggy and pretends to struggle.

"Okay, enough," Iggy cried. Thankfully, Hugo stopped. It sounded like Iggy cleared his throat. "Joey then scratches Hugo. To fight back, Hugo picks up a rock and smashes Joey on the back of the head. Voilà." Iggy faced his friend. "No need to demonstrate that part."

They were too cute together. "I have to say, I am impressed, Detective Iggy."

"Is he always like this?" Maddy asked with awe in her voice.

"Yes. We are kind of a crime solving family."

She smiled. "I can see why you and my son get along so well. Jaxson always had an analytical mind."

"As does Drake." Actually, Drake might be more analytical than Jaxson, but it was a close call.

"I agree. They take after their dad."

Maddy was so sweet.

"Oh, I forgot. I need to warn you all about something." She sounded tense.

"Warn us about what?"

"The sheriff's department is checking everybody who came to Maddy's party."

"Checking for what?" Maddy asked.

Genevieve looked down at Hugo who was still on the floor. He lifted Iggy off his chest and stood.

"Checking for what, Genevieve?" Maddy asked again.

"Sorry. I don't know. I mean, I watched as the deputy stuck this swab thingy in the person's mouth, but I don't know what it was for."

I could figure it out. "Jane sure isn't wasting any time working this forty-year old cold case, now is she? And yet she hasn't made a lot of progress on Armand's murder."

"I think what you said before is right, Glinda," Jaxson said. "The two cases are connected somehow—and Jane thinks so, too. Solve one, and you can figure out the other."

"That's assuming the killer is from Magnolia. Genevieve found out Joey Franklin was from Citrus Park, which is not very far from here," Maddy said.

"Another scenario is that Joey Franklin had a date. Driving to Magnolia wouldn't be a big deal if the two towns are close. They go to the fair, which back then would have been a big deal," I said. "Maybe they were enjoying the festivities when they decided to explore another part of the park. Things got heated. He attacked her, and she fought back."

Maddy shook her head. "Glinda, you are amazing. Your imagination is impressive."

I wasn't sure if I should take that as a compliment or not. "Thank you?"

She smiled. "It's a great trait to have. Together, the three of you make a formidable unit."

Iggy twisted in Hugo's grasp, and the big guy set him on the coffee table. "We are good, aren't we?" Iggy said, his chest elevated. "Glinda and Jaxson wouldn't have been able to solve most of the cases without my help, though." He looked over at Hugo. "Okay, fine. Hugo and Genevieve help a lot, too."

I swallowed a smile as Pete stepped closer to Iggy and then faced me and Jaxson. "I bet you all could use a flying, cloaking bird to help solve crimes, couldn't you?"

I couldn't imagine what would happen if we added Pete to the mix of crime solvers. He might prove very useful as a fly on the wall, but he and Iggy would try to one up each other all the time, and that wouldn't be healthy. "I'm sure Maddy and Eugene would miss you too much if you moved back to Witch's Cove with us."

"We would. You are ours, Pete," Maddy said.

He flapped his wings. "Fine, but you have to promise to talk to me like I'm one of you once the spell wears off. And I want to have some outdoor time to fly around too. I won't leave. I promise. I like getting free food and maid service too much."

We all smiled. "I promise," Maddy said.

"Getting back to your idea, Glinda," Jaxson said. "If the person who killed Joey was a woman—possibly his date—and I'm not saying it was, who would have dug the grave? I'm not trying to be sexist, but I don't think the woman in your scenario would have the wherewithal or physical ability to locate a shovel and dig for a few hours."

"Not unless she called a male friend to help."

We sat there in silence for a few minutes and then tossed around a few more theories, but there were no facts to back up any of it.

"Maybe the two crimes aren't connected," Jaxson said. "How about we redirect our efforts to Armand's death? I know Pete claims the fairgrounds are involved, but what if it's all about infidelity?"

"That might be easier. The Franklin case has too many unknowns." I picked up the list of attendees and read through the names. "Let's suppose that Trixie is Bea Jones, Daniel Lee's wife. If she wanted to be with Armand, she might know who wanted him dead," I said.

"Lydia comes to mind," Maddy said.

"Or Bea's husband, Daniel Lee. He might want to get rid of the competition, just like Genevieve suggested," I said.

"Seems to me like a lot of folks had a grudge against Armand," Eugene said. "First and foremost, would be Lydia. She was angry at him for having an affair with Bea—assuming she is the girlfriend. If not Lydia, then

Bea's husband, Daniel Lee. He can't be happy with Armand for being with his wife. And thirdly, I can't help but go back to Mary Jo and Sharon. They've never wavered in trying to stop Armand and Daniel Lee from wanting to put in that strip mall where the fairgrounds is."

"Excellent synopsis, Eugene. I can see where your sons get their deductive reasoning skills." He smiled. "I think we need to talk with Lydia." I looked over at Maddy. She was the one who thought it wasn't a good idea to disturb the grieving widow.

"Ask away," Maddy said. "It seems as if I was fooled by her hysterics. She might be in the middle of this. If you do question her, I suggest you don't accuse her of killing her husband right away. She'll shut down real fast. I think if we find out whether Bea Jones is Trixie, it may be good enough."

I had more sense than to alienate someone. "I'm okay with that, though I wonder if Jane already knows Trixie's identity. Magnolia is a small town. I imagine there's someone here who would know about Bea and Armand."

"Lizzy Davenport," Iggy said.

"How do you know that?" I asked.

"Hugo said Lizzy was talking with Lydia after her husband was killed. Don't you remember? They were chatting on the phone."

If my familiar remembered more details than I did, I

should start taking notes. “I forgot.” I turned to Eugene. “You said she’s a receptionist at the courthouse, right?”

“Yes.”

“Do you think you could ask her who this Trixie women is?”

Eugene slapped his hand on his chest. “Me? An old man gossiping about a woman having an affair? No, thank you.” He glanced to the side. “But, I know of someone who might be willing to do a little undercover work for me.”

“Great,” I said.

“I’ll head into work tomorrow and ask her.”

“Eugene, I thought you were going to stay home until all of this mess was over?” Maddy said as she clasped his hand.

“I’ll be careful.”

“Dad, I’ll go with you to work,” Jaxson said. “You can show me around the courthouse. No one will dare try anything if you aren’t alone.”

Eugene smiled. “Good. We’ll go first thing tomorrow morning.”

“That’s great,” I said. “Let’s suppose we learn that Bea is this Trixie woman. Then what? Since she has no reason to kill Armand, we could just ask for her help. She might have an idea who wanted him dead.”

Genevieve stood. “Hugo and I can find out.”

They were gone before we could stop them. A few

seconds later, the doorbell rang. Jaxson jumped up and answered it. "Deputy."

He led him inside. "The sheriff wants to collect everyone's DNA." He explained why.

"I wasn't alive when that man was killed," I said. "And neither was Jaxson. Nor are we from here."

"I know, ma'am, but the sheriff insists that we test everyone who was at the Christmas party."

"That will be quite an expense." I honestly didn't know the cost, but it wouldn't be cheap to run twenty or thirty samples.

"She will only process a few at a time."

Whatever. "Fine."

The deputy took cheek swabs from us all. I was thankful that Genevieve and Hugo weren't here. The lab would freak if they found two sets of DNA that weren't human.

The young man seemed a bit embarrassed at having to do this, but I didn't mind. I just hoped it would reveal something useful. The person Joey Franklin had scratched would have to be quite old by now.

When the deputy left, I could feel the relief permeate the room. "This might be the final step in learning who killed Joey Franklin," I said.

Eugene stood and walked over to the sideboard that held some liquor bottles. "Even if we learn that Joey was killed by Mr. ABC or Ms. ABC, how does that help us find the person who killed Armand?"

He poured himself and Maddy a glass of scotch. I looked over at Jaxson.

"Dad, speculating won't do us any good. Trust me. This Joey Franklin deserves an answer, even though he's gone. I'm betting the sheriff is looking for his relatives as we speak."

"Maybe."

Even though it hadn't been long since our two teleporters had left, they both appeared.

"Yes," Genevieve said.

"Yes to what?" I asked.

"Bea Jones is Trixie." She lifted her chin, clearly proud of herself.

"How did you find that out?" Maddy asked.

"Hugo went back to visit Lydia—cloaked, of course—and I went to see Lizzy. Don't ask me how I found out where she lived. Okay, I looked in Lydia's phone first, and then went over to Lizzy's. They don't live very far from each other." She smiled. "I'm getting quite good with electronics if I do say so myself."

"Both of the women said Trixie was Bea?" Eugene asked.

Genevieve blew out a breath. "Indirectly. Okay. The truth? Hugo kind of suggested to Lydia that she call Lizzy and talk about Trixie."

Iggy perked up. "See? Hugo can do anything."

More hero worship. "Thank you both for clarifying."

"So now what?" Jaxson said. "All this proves is that

Bea Jones was having an affair with Armand Linfield. His wife found out. If Lydia wanted to kill someone, I would think she'd kill Bea, not her own husband."

He had a point. "I guess we'll have to wait until the sheriff solves the Joey Franklin case to learn something more about Armand's situation."

"I guess so."

Jaxson and I had debated returning to Witch's Cove for a few days, or maybe a few weeks, since it would probably take that long to process so many DNA samples. Joey Franklin's DNA had been done quickly, but the sheriff had a lot more than one sample to process this time.

In the end, we decided to stay and enjoy what Magnolia had to offer for a few days, since Jaxson wasn't from there either. He first took me to a used bookstore, which was such a delight. We then stopped at an amazing bakery before taking in Magnolia's small historical museum. To our delight, there were some old photos of the fairgrounds when they first opened. If I'd lived back then, I would have loved going to the fair.

Jaxson's cell rang just as we were leaving the museum. "It's my dad." He answered. "Yeah, Dad. What's up? She did? Who was it? No, I've never met her. Sure, we'll head home now." Jaxson disconnected.

"Well?"

"The DNA results came back. The results showed that the person Joey Franklin scratched was someone related to Bea Jones."

"I wouldn't have guessed that. I know that person couldn't be Bea since she's only about forty. So who was it? Her mom or dad?"

"My father didn't know."

"I wonder how he found out? I thought Jane didn't leak information," I said.

"He didn't say."

It didn't take us long to return to his parents' house. When we entered, we found Wilson Eberhart, their nosy neighbor, having a scotch with Eugene and Maddy. Ten bucks said he was the leak.

The older gentleman smiled. "Nice to see you again, Glinda."

There was something about him that was a bit creepy, but it was probably because my imagination was on overload. "You, too."

Jaxson and I sat down on the sofa across from Jaxson's parents and their neighbor.

"Go ahead, Wilson. Tell them what you told us," Eugene said.

He clasped his hands and then looked right then left. "Let's just say that I have a *friend* in the sheriff's department. He told me that the person Joey Franklin scratched was either a sister or the mother of Bea Jones."

"A female. Good to know. What did Bea say about it?" I asked.

Wilson pressed his lips together and slightly shook his head. "My friend said Bea claimed she had no idea about anything, but I don't believe her."

"Why? What do you know?" It was clear he was hiding something.

"I knew her sister, Aurora, back when we were in high school. In those days, everyone dated around. But guess who she dated for a short while?"

The man was worse than Genevieve in telling a story. "Who?"

"Sid Harper."

Needless to say, my spidey senses shot up. "Bea's sister dated Sid Harper?"

"Yup."

Considering the town of Magnolia wasn't much larger than Witch's Cove, the class size couldn't be very large. "Interesting."

He lifted his hand. "But...here's the thing. It wasn't long after they broke up that Aurora and her parents moved away."

"Do you mean Aurora, Bea, and her parents?" I asked.

He smiled. "No. Bea wouldn't be born for another six months."

"Where is the family now?"

"The Plummers moved to someplace in Georgia, but I don't know where she is living now—assuming she's still alive."

"Do you think Aurora killed Joey Franklin?" I asked. "Then, not wanting to be around if people started questioning this man's disappearance, the family decided it would be best to move away?" My conspiracy theory ideas were running rampant in my head.

"I have no idea what happened," Wilson said. "If I were the sheriff, though, I'd find Aurora and ask her what really happened forty years ago at the fairgrounds."

"That would be useful." I turned to Maddy. "No one brought a guest to your party, like Bea's sister or anything, did they?"

"No. There were no guests."

That eliminated Aurora or her mom from having killed Armand. I might be talked into believing that the two cases weren't connected other than the fact that Sid Harper was dating the woman who was attacked that night. It seemed unlikely that she could have killed Joey Franklin, though. If she was in high school, she couldn't have been more than eighteen.

While this was great information, I wasn't sure it helped us figure out who killed Armand Linfield.

CHAPTER FOURTEEN

"MR. EBERHART, please thank your source for us. This information opens up a lot of possibilities," I said.

"I will." He stood. "I need to get back. If I hear anything else, I'll let you know."

Once the neighbor left, my head spun. "What are you all thinking?" I asked.

"I'm thinking we need Genevieve and Hugo to get back here," Jaxson said.

"You have me," Iggy said.

"And me too." Pete ruffled his feathers. "What good does it do for everyone to hear me if I can't do anything?"

Now he sounded like Iggy.

As if our wish was our command, our two gargoyle shifters instantly appeared. "You're here!" I said, happy for the distraction since I had no answer for poor Pete.

"We've been here. We thought it would be better if the sheriff's department and the neighbor guy didn't know we exist."

That was very mature of her. "Good thinking."

"Hugo and I are going to split up."

I stiffened. "What?"

"That didn't come out right. I mean, we're going to do that divide and conquer thing again. I'm going to see what Sid Harper is up to, and Hugo will check out Bea Jones, aka, Trixie."

"That's good thinking. Maybe I'm way off base, but could Aurora and Sid Harper be Bea Jones' biological parents?"

Eugene huffed out a laugh. "They were in high school when they dated. They were just kids."

He sure was innocent. I looked over at Maddy. "Maybe those novels I've read exaggerated things, but something like sixty years ago, teenagers who became pregnant were often sent to a home for unwed mothers or else the whole family moved. Once the baby was born, the child was either put up for adoption or the girls' mother pretended as if the baby was her own. Am I right?"

Maddy bit down on her lip. "Yes, but I can't believe Sid or Bea would have been able to keep that a secret for this long."

Iggy crawled onto the table. That was his platform for delivering some insightful news. "What if they don't know? Or rather Sid didn't know. Not that I really understand how that stuff works, but Aurora might not have told him."

Maddy shrugged. "It's possible. Most wouldn't question Bea being Aurora's sister. Women do have children sixteen or seventeen years apart, especially if they started having kids at a young age. It's not common, though."

I looked around. "How do we find out who Bea's mother was, other than from our two teleporting friends?"

"I have a few lawyer friends," Eugene said. "Maybe they can find Bea's birth certificate."

"I imagine Jane knows the answer or will know shortly."

"Can I fly someplace to see what's happening?" Pete asked.

"Maybe," Jaxson said. "But we need to find a destination first, okay?"

"Fine."

"I have an idea," Maddy said. "There is a woman who lives down the street. She's in her seventies and used to be an English teacher here at the high school. If my math is right, she could have taught Aurora, Wilson, Sid, Mary Jo, or Sharon. She might know something."

"That great. I can't remember, was she at the Christmas party?"

"No, Louisa was out of town."

"I see," I said. "You know, I only taught middle school for a year, but often the kids acted as if I wasn't even in the same room as them. They would say things in front of me they shouldn't have. Do you think you can invite her over? Maybe for dinner tonight?"

Maddy grinned. "That is a great idea. Let me call Louisa. If she says yes, I'll have Eugene pick up some takeout."

I didn't like the idea of him leaving the house. "Jaxson and I can grab something."

"Perfect. I'll call her now." Maddy went into the kitchen. I guess she'd left her phone in there. When she returned a few minutes later, she was smiling. "It's all set. Louisa Netburn will be here at six."

We discussed what Maddy wanted to serve. Since it was nearly five, we needed to pick up the food soon. Eugene called in an order, and a little while later, Jaxson and I drove to town to get it.

"Do you have any theories as to what might have happened at the fairgrounds?" I asked Jaxson as soon as we were in the truck.

"No. How would I?"

"Guess," I urged. It's what we usually did.

"Okay, other than the fact that Aurora, whose last name we don't know, was there, I'd need more to go on. Like was she with Sid? But if I had been her high school boyfriend, I wouldn't have let her go there by herself at night. Even if the fair was going gangbusters, there is a lot of property where an assault could happen without anyone noticing."

I loved his protective nature. "Let's suppose that Aurora was with Sid, and that she was attacked by Joey Franklin. Why didn't Sid step in right away? To me, considering that Joey was able to claw her, it almost implies she was alone."

Jaxson pulled to a stop at a light. "Many of the guys in my high school lacked muscles. Joey, who the doctor guessed was in his early twenties at the time, might have been a bit more buff."

"What are you saying?" I asked. "That Sid Harper watched some guy attack his girlfriend and did nothing because he was afraid of getting beaten up?"

"Maybe. Considering that Joey was hit in the back of the head with a rock, Sid might have picked up a heavy stone, snuck up behind him, and hit Joey instead of engaging in hand-to-hand combat."

"And the blow to the head killed him," I added. "He must have used one big rock."

"Most likely," Jaxson said.

"This implies Sid might be our fairground killer. Do you think he didn't turn himself in because he thought he'd be charged with a crime?" I asked.

Jaxson shrugged. "It wasn't exactly self-defense, unless he thought he'd be next, or if he thought his girlfriend might have been killed. If someone was trying to harm you, I'd kill the guy."

"Thank you. I guess it matters whether Joey Franklin was merely trying to rob her or if he wanted to physically harm her. In any case, I would think Sid would have been cleared, especially if he was a juvenile, but I can't say for sure."

"I took a few law classes in college, but I don't recall learning about this kind of stuff," he said.

We parked in the To-Go slot at the restaurant. A few minutes later, a server came out with our meal, and the rich aroma of the lasagna had my taste buds salivating. Jaxson paid and we took off. "Do you think this Louisa Netburn remembers students from forty years ago?"

Jaxson smiled. "I wish I had all the answers, pink lady, but I don't. We'll find out soon, though."

Once back at the house, we went inside with the food. No one was in the living room, but from the clatter in the kitchen, that was where we'd find Jaxson's mom.

"Food's here." I placed the bags on the counter. "How can I help?"

"There are some serving dishes in the cupboard under the counter. If you can get out three of them, that would be great. When Louisa arrives, I'll serve the food."

"Okay." Once I found what Maddy needed, Jaxson and I set the table.

Eugene, who'd been in his office when we first came

home, left to fetch their neighbor. He promised he'd be safe walking four houses down the street. I had the sense Jaxson wanted to escort his dad, but he understood his father was a proud man. Thankfully, Eugene returned safely with Louisa Netburn a few minutes later.

The school teacher wasn't at all what I expected. If she was seventy-three, I wanted her secret to youth. Her dark auburn hair was pulled back in a ponytail, and her blue jeans fit her slim body. Her face was almost devoid of makeup, yet that seemed to enhance her beauty.

Maddy came out of the kitchen and rushed up to her friend. "Louisa, thanks for coming over. I want you to meet my son and his fiancée."

Jaxson had asked that I not grill the poor woman, and while I agreed that I could be a little over-the-top, we needed answers. But, I would do the best I could.

Maddy led us to the dining room, and then she and Eugene carried out the food.

"This is so lovely, Maddy. I get tired of fast food."

Louisa didn't look like she ate anything unhealthy. Once we'd chosen our food, Maddy asked Louisa about her children and grandkids and what they were up to. While interesting, I wanted to talk about the important stuff.

To my delight, it was Eugene who brought up the

dead body. "Did you hear about the man who was found buried on the fairground property?" he asked.

"Oh, my yes. It's all anyone is talking about. What have you heard?"

Bless her heart. She loved to gossip, too.

Eugene detailed what little information we had, leaving out some pieces that we only found out about because of Genevieve and Hugo's snooping. "Our neighbor told us that the woman Joey Franklin scratched during the attack was a relative of Bea Jones."

She sucked in a breath. "I had no idea. Was it her sister, Aurora?"

Interesting that she should bring up her name.

"We belicve so," Maddy said. "Did you teach her?"

"For a year. Then she and her parents moved away, I think to Georgia."

"Who was she friends with?" Eugene asked.

It was almost as if he'd read my mind.

"She, Mary Jo Henderson, and Sharon Dillup were best friends."

"I take it Mary Jo Henderson is now Mary Jo Harper, and Sharon is now Sharon Graeber?" I asked.

Louisa smiled. "Oh, yes. I still think of them as eighteen and unmarried."

I could relate. I'd not run into any of my old students, but in my mind they would be forever eighth graders.

I wish I could take notes. If Aurora was at the fairgrounds with Sid, were her best friends nearby? When I was in high school, we would travel in packs—the girlfriends along with their boyfriends.

"I heard that Aurora was dating Sid Harper before he dated Mary Jo." I know I shouldn't be asking questions or making statements like that, but this former school teacher seemed anxious to share. I could sense a gossip when I met one.

"She was." Louisa looked upward, as if she was trying to retrieve some memory. "I believe Sid started dating Mary Jo the year after Aurora moved away."

"Do you know why Aurora's family left Magnolia?" I wouldn't call this snooping. I'd call it being interested in another person's life. Fine. I like to tell myself what I wanted to believe.

"I never asked."

That ended that conversation—at least for me. If I started pressing the issue, Louisa would wonder why I was being so noisy.

"So were Mary Jo, Sharon, and Aurora tight?" Eugene asked.

I wonder what part of being best friends he didn't understand, or was he fishing for more information?

"What is this about?" Louisa asked.

I wasn't going to answer that. Thankfully, Maddy launched into the fact that Armand Linfield, who was on the City Council with Mary Jo and Sharon, was murdered in their house. I wasn't sure how that answered Louisa's question about why we wanted to know the relationship between the three girls, but Louisa didn't ask any more questions about why he wanted to know.

"I did hear about that tragedy. Do they know who killed this man?" Louisa asked.

"No, but there might be a connection between his death and the man found in a grave at the fairgrounds," he told her.

Louisa's eyes widened. "Oh, I see. How can I help?"

I liked this woman. For the rest of the meal we batted around some theories. I wasn't about to speculate how the two cases were connected, except that Mary Jo and Sharon could have been at both murder scenes. I was pretty sure that if Sheriff Waters asked those two ladies, they'd deny it, though.

Since we didn't want to make this dinner about murder, Maddy eventually steered the conversation to Louisa's new gardening hobby. We were about to have dessert when an idea struck.

"Louisa, who else did Aurora hang out with else besides Mary Jo and Sharon?" It was possible Aurora might have confided in a friend about what happen that fateful night at the fairgrounds.

"It's been what, forty years? I'm sorry to say, after a while, the names and faces blend together, but if you could find a copy of an old yearbook, that might give you a clue."

She was a genius. "We might do that."

After dessert, Louisa said it was getting close to her bedtime, and since it was dark, both Eugene and Jaxson escorted Louisa home. In the few minutes they were gone, I helped Maddy clean up. "What do you think?" I asked.

"About?"

"This Aurora woman was of the age to have tangled with Joey Franklin. Whether she killed him or say, Sid Harper, killed him, she was involved in this."

"I'm sure Jane is investigating."

"Yes, but Jane doesn't have jurisdiction in Atlanta, where we think Aurora lives."

"Just because she moved there when she was sixteen, doesn't mean Aurora is there now."

Maddy was just like her son—always poking holes in my theories. "You're right. We could ask Bea, but she'd wonder why we wanted to know."

The front door opened and both men returned. I went out to the living room since we'd just finished cleaning up. "Hey. Maddy and I were—or rather I was—wondering if Aurora still lives in Georgia or if she'd moved in the last forty years. Do you think you could do a search for her?" I asked Jaxson.

"Sure. Do we know her last name?"

"Wilson told us her maiden name was Plummer but she probably married and has a different last name now."

Jaxson smiled. "I can work with that. We know she is around fifty-six, fifty-seven years old, right?"

"That's assuming Joey died exactly forty years ago. If the site lists siblings, her sister would be Beatrix Plummer Jones."

"Got it."

Jaxson disappeared into the bedroom, and once he returned with his laptop, he dropped down onto the sofa and fired up his computer.

It took him less than ten minutes to find Aurora Plummer's name. "Got it. Her name is Aurora Belfrey now, and she lives in Tampa. These sites are often out of date, though."

"That means Jane Waters might need to ask for help from their police department if she wants to find out what Aurora knows."

"Assuming Aurora isn't willing to voluntarily do a tell-all," Jaxson said.

I twisted toward him. "True. And even if your sheriff questions Mary Jo and Sharon about the night their good friend was attacked, they will probably say they weren't with her, even if they were."

"Maybe, but Jane has to realize that if the three of them were such good friends that even if they weren't at the fairgrounds with her that night, they would have heard what happened to Aurora."

"Exactly, so why haven't they come forward? Huh?"

Eugene finished fixing his drink. "I don't like any of

this. This town doesn't need city officials hiding something like this. I know it happened forty years ago, but still."

We discussed a bit more about this new information from the neighbor when Genevieve and Hugo appeared.

"Phew. We have had fun," she said.

"Fun? I thought you were investigating a murder or two."

She waved a hand. "We did, but since we ended up in Tampa, we thought we'd explore Ybor City and their new football and baseball stadium."

"Tampa? Why did you go there?" How had they learned that Aurora lived there now? Oh right. They probably spied on Jane.

Genevieve tilted her head to the side. "Jane found out that Aurora lives there. She asked their police department to bring her in for questioning. I'm surprised she didn't go there herself, but it would be faster this way, I guess."

I was impressed with Jane Waters, as well as with Genevieve and Hugo for following up. "And did they learn anything interesting?"

"Yup."

CHAPTER FIFTEEN

I WAITED for Genevieve to get to the point, but she just stood there smiling. "And?" I asked.

"Oh, right. Well, we first stopped by the police department. Boy, is that a big place. Compared to the Witch's Cove sheriff's department, Tampa has a lot of officers."

We were getting off track. "Yes, Tampa is a big city. Witch's Cove is not. But these murders happened in Magnolia. Can we focus, please?"

She looked over at Hugo and then inhaled. "Sure. At the request of Sheriff Waters, the Tampa Police called in Aurora Belfrey—that's her married name. She said she knew this day was coming, but she was hoping it would be another forty years before they dug up the body."

"Did she say what happened?"

"Yup. She's claiming self-defense."

We needed a bit more detail than that. "She's admitting to having killed Joey Franklin?"

"Not exactly."

"What exactly did she say? Was she claiming that Joey attacked her, and fearing for her life, she hit him with a rock? And did she say why was she in the park alone that night? Or wasn't she alone? Details, please."

Genevieve straightened. "Got it. Okay. No, she was not alone. Aurora had gone to the fair with her boyfriend, and you'll never guess who that was."

"Sid Harper."

Her chin tucked in. "You know?"

At this rate, we'd never get answers. "Yes. Go on."

"Well, Sid needed to um...relieve himself, so they went to some wooded area. While Aurora was giving Sid some privacy, this Joey guy grabbed her from behind. She struggled, but he was too powerful for her and ended up knocking her to the ground."

"Is that when Sid realized what was happening and rushed to help her?" Jaxson asked.

"More or less. Aurora showed the police the scars on her thighs from where Joey dug his nails into her leg."

"That fits what the forensic anthropologist found. That's good," I said. "Then what happened?"

"After she screamed, Sid came running. She started crying that this man was going to kill her. It was really sad. I don't like to see sad people," Genevieve said.

I appreciated that she was an empathetic person, but I wanted to get to the killing part—not because I enjoyed hearing about it, but because I wanted to know exactly what Sid did. "That's really nice. What did Sid do next?"

"All Aurora knew was that the guy went limp on top of her. Apparently, Sid hit the guy with a rock. Once. She said he didn't mean to kill the guy. He just wanted him to leave her alone."

"That makes sense." I looked over at Iggy, who was looking upward. I swear if he could whistle, he would be. "That's what Iggy said happened. Then what did they do?"

"Aurora wanted to call the police, but Sid thought he might be sent to jail. He was only seventeen, and he was scared. He didn't know if he'd committed a crime or not."

"So Sid buried the body?" Jaxson asked.

"Yes, but only after he called his best high school friend to help."

Iggy nodded. "It was Clive Graeber," he said, clearly receiving the information from Hugo. Even her *mate* seemed impatient to get to the end of the story.

"Sharon's husband and Mary Jo's husband buried the body?" I didn't see that coming.

"Yes."

Jaxson leaned forward. "Aurora thought her life was

in danger. Why? Did she say if her attacker had a knife or a gun?"

"Oh, yes. I forgot that part," Genevieve said.

Sometimes I wanted to strangle her, but without her talents, we wouldn't have learned this much. "Which was it?"

"He had a knife that he'd pressed against her throat, but he didn't have the chance to use it—or else he never planned to kill her in the first place."

"What did Sid and Clive do with this knife?" Eugene asked.

"Sid took the knife—or so Aurora claimed."

"Let's hope he still has it to show that he feared Aurora would be killed," I said.

She shrugged. "I don't know."

Pete flew over to the table. "Let me get inside his house. Assuming I still have the ability to see through walls and things, I might be able to look around his place and find this weapon—that is, if Sid kept it for forty years."

That would be great, but it wasn't really my call.

"Pete," Maddy said. "It could be dangerous. Sid and Mary Jo live in the house. Besides, how would you even get in?"

"Hugo can take me inside. I can cloak myself if they are there."

Hugo turned to Genevieve who translated for him.

"Don't worry about Pete. He can sit on Hugo's shoulder. If Hugo is cloaked, Pete will be, too."

I had to remember that, though I couldn't imagine sitting on Hugo's shoulders. I had been able to cloak myself in the past, but it required a long spell and took a lot out of me.

"What do you think?" Maddy asked Eugene.

"If Sid and Mary Jo are at work tomorrow, it might be safer, but would he still have the knife after all this time?" Eugene said.

Jaxson held up his hand. "Let's suppose he does. Even if Pete finds a knife, I'm not sure how he'll know if it was the knife from a crime forty years ago or if it's some hunting knife Sid owns."

"Or one of Mary Jo's butcher knives," Maddy tossed in.

"True, and it's not like Hugo can just take it. If he did, it would be inadmissible as evidence."

Sometimes, I hated the law. "If you thought you might have committed a crime, would you have kept the knife?" I asked Jaxson. "We're talking about a teenager, remember?"

"Probably not, but if Jane arrests Sid, we need to make sure she asks about it," Jaxson said.

"Sounds good," Eugene said.

"I should be happy that we found out who killed Joey Franklin, but what about Armand? Do we still think the two cases are related?" I asked.

"I imagine that if Sid and Clive buried the body that Aurora would have told her two best friends, Mary Jo and Sharon, about it," Jaxson said.

"If she didn't, I hope that Sid and Clive told their wives about their secret at some point in the last forty years," I said. "Desiring to protect their husbands from being dragged into a murder investigation, Mary Jo and Sharon worked really hard to keep developers out of that area. It finally makes sense."

Eugene's cell rang. When he checked the caller ID, his face paled. "It's the Mayor."

That didn't sound good.

Eugene answered. "Yes, Mr. Mayor." He listened for a good thirty seconds. "Oh, really? I can't believe that. Are you sure he's guilty?"

I grabbed Jaxson's hand. Had the sheriff cracked the Armand Linfield case?

After a few questions, Eugene hung up. "Our sheriff didn't waste any time. She arrested Sid Harper for Joey Franklin's murder."

"Based on what Aurora told the Tampa Police, he sounded innocent—at least to me."

"Me, too."

"Aurora told the Tampa Police that after the attack, they decided it would be best if they didn't keep in contact anymore. That mean she didn't know whether he tossed the knife or not," Genevieve said.

"What does Sid claim?" I asked.

"The Mayor didn't say."

"Dad, why did the Mayor call you?"

"He wants me to come in tomorrow. Mary Jo is taking a leave of absence, and I'm her substitute."

"What about Sharon Graeber?" I asked.

"What about her?"

"Her husband helped bury the guy. He should be guilty of something. Though if the crime happened forty-years ago, there might be a statute of limitations for that," I said.

"I'm sure that when I go into work tomorrow, I'll learn more. There will only be me, Daniel Lee, and Sharon on the Council now." He shook his head. "This is bad."

"I'm sorry, Dad."

Maddy stood. "I'll fix us something to snack on. It could be a long night of discussion."

When no one said anything, Maddy went about doing her thing—which was to make everyone else happy.

"What do you think will happen to Sid?" I asked. "He was a juvenile, but not contacting the police right away will look bad for him."

"I agree," Eugene said. "This town doesn't need any more scandals. Let's hope Sid kept that knife."

A few minutes later, Maddy carried out a plate of veggies and a bowl of chips and dip. When Eugene reached for the chips, Maddy lowered her gaze and slightly shook her head. Eugene shot her a look and then grabbed a handful of the veggies.

"Does anyone think Sid killed Armand, even if he had reason to believe that Armand might achieve his goal of having a developer come in and build a mall?" I asked.

"I would have said absolutely not, until we learned what happened all those years ago," Maddy said.

"Do you think the sheriff can get a warrant to search Sid's home for a syringe or for that liquid pesticide?" I asked.

"Jane is a persistent person," Eugene said. "If she wants something, she'll get it."

"Do you want me and Hugo to ask Sid about that night?" Genevieve said.

"How? Do you plan to pop up inside a jail cell and hope no one notices there are three people in there? Please don't. It would cause more of a scandal than a teenage boy trying to protect his girlfriend."

"Fine, but we want to help."

I appreciated her desire to do something. Heck, I wanted to help too. I turned to Jaxson. "When you were a teenager, if there was something you absolutely didn't want your dad to find, where would you have hid it?"

"That depends on whether I wanted to retrieve it quickly."

"What do you mean?" I asked.

Jaxson glanced over at his father. "If it was reading

material I knew my dad wouldn't approve of, I hid it under my mattress. That way, I could access it easily."

"But if you had something you wanted to stash away for a long time, like a knife or a gun, where would you have put it?"

Jaxson dipped his chin. "I never had a gun in high school, but if I *found* a gun and wanted to get rid of it, I would have buried it in my backyard."

I grabbed a handful of chips. "That doesn't help. If Sid buried Joey Franklin's knife in his backyard, the new owners could have paved over the yard by now."

"No," Eugene said. "Sid and Mary Jo live in Sid's family home. When his parents passed, Sid inherited the home, or should I say their mansion."

My pulse soared. "Are you saying the knife could still be in the family's backyard—assuming Sid buried it there?"

"It could be, but it's not like we can go looking for it."

Before I could voice my suggestion, the doorbell rang. Eugene looked over at Maddy. "Are you expecting anyone?"

"Not me."

The fact Hugo and Genevieve had disappeared implied it might be the sheriff again. Eugene answered the door. "Clive? This is a surprise. Come in."

Clive Graeber, Sharon's husband and fellow grave

digger, walked in. His fists were clenched, and his jaw was definitely tight.

"Can I get you something to drink?" Eugene asked.

He nodded to the glasses on the table. "Whatever you're having."

Jaxson jumped up. "I'll fix it."

"Come and sit down, unless you want to talk to me in private," Eugene said.

"No. In fact, I need to speak with everyone." He glanced over at Pete who was sitting on the back of the sofa, acting as if it was his home. "Including your bird."

"Pete?" Eugene asked.

"Yes." Clive sat down. "I heard a rumor that your bird has some kind of X-ray vision ability."

Oh, boy. We didn't need that to go viral.

"How did you hear about that?" Eugene asked.

"I'd rather not name names, but let's say I know people in high places."

Ouch. I bet Jane Waters would be unhappy to learn there was another leak in her department.

"I see," Eugene said.

"Is it true that your bird found the body at the fairgrounds?" Clive asked.

"Yes, he did," Eugene said.

"You should know that he might not have that ability anymore," I interjected. "My friend and I put a spell on him, but it was only supposed to last for a short period of time."

"But he might still have it, right?" Poor Clive sounded so hopeful.

"Yes. Why?"

"I figure if he could find a buried body, your bird can find a buried knife."

Ah. I wanted to ask which knife he was talking about, but it would be too hard to explain how we learned that information.

"What knife?" Eugene asked. The man could have won an award for keeping a straight face.

"I don't know how much you know about what happened that night at the fairgrounds," Clive said, "and why that man had to die."

"The Mayor just called me and told me quite a lot."

"Okay. Did he tell you that Sid thought this man was going to kill Aurora, his girlfriend? Since Sid was pretty scrawny back then—not to mention a nerd—he was smart enough to realize that a physical confrontation would have ended badly for him. Very badly."

"What did he do?" Eugene asked.

"I wasn't there, but he told me what happened. He was in the woods doing his business when he heard Aurora screaming for help. Sid said he was scared. Really scared, but he loved Aurora and wanted to save her. When he rushed to help her, he stumbled over a rock. That's when it hit him—no pun intended. He bent down and dug the rock out of the ground. In the meantime, Aurora was pleading with the guy to get off her."

"I can't imagine what was going through Sid's mind. I would have frozen," I said.

"Sid almost did, but when he finally freed the rock, he raced up to the guy. When he saw the knife to Aurora's throat, Sid didn't think. He just smashed the man's skull in. Literally."

"How horrible." I was serious. "The law might think differently, but I would have done the same thing."

"Me too," Clive said.

"Then what did he do?" Jaxson asked.

"All Sid could think of was to get rid of the body. Aurora's leg was bleeding where she'd been scratched, and she was crying hysterically. She told him she'd be okay and to do what he needed to do to make everything go away."

"Why didn't he call the police?" I couldn't help but ask.

Clive shook his head. "He was a teenager. He knew he'd killed someone and didn't want to go to jail. He believed his action was justified, but he was no lawyer."

"I bet adrenaline was coursing through his body." Mine would have been.

"He was definitely a mess. Since he needed help, he called me and asked if I would bring two shovels. He wouldn't say why. Being his best friend, I did. Once I saw what happened, I told him to tell the cops, but he said he didn't want to get me in trouble." Clive dipped his head. "So, I helped dig the grave once Sid explained what the man did to Aurora. I have no doubt that her attacker would have killed her."

"Did you see the knife?" Jaxson asked.

"I did."

As a teenager, Sid might not have had the wherewithal to use a cloth or something to pick it up. "Did he grab the knife and carry it back to his car or something?"

"Believe it or not, he took off his T-shirt and wrapped the knife in it."

"Where is this knife now?" Eugene asked.

"I had no idea until today, because I never asked. The less I knew the better. A little while ago, I went to the jail to see him, and Sid finally told me that he'd buried the knife in his yard. I asked him where, but he doesn't remember exactly. All he knows for sure is that it's buried somewhere near a tree. The problem is that over the years, his parents moved trees and relandscaped the yard, so it could be anywhere back there. There are a few acres of lawn. Sid would look, but he can't from jail."

My sympathy for Sid rose. "He asked you to locate it, didn't he?"

"He did."

"Clive, out of curiosity, do you remember the date of the attack?" Eugene asked.

"Remember? Are you kidding? I still have nightmares about it. It was April 19, 1983." He stabbed a hand over his nearly bald head.

"Does your wife know what happened?" I asked.

"She does. It's why she and Mary Jo were so against the land being developed. They feared, rightfully so, that the construction process might expose the body."

The pieces were finally falling into place.

"What can we do?" Eugene asked.

"When I heard about how your bird found the body, I thought maybe he could help Sid find this knife. That would prove that Sid isn't a murderer."

"Pete," Eugene said. "Do you want to give it a go?"

"Are you kidding? Of course, I do."

Iggy crawled onto my lap. I could tell he was feeling a bit left out. "I know Ruby isn't here to make sure Pete can do this, but we should take Iggy with us too," I said. "He can help maintain Pete's magic." Yes, I totally made that up, but there was a sliver of a chance it was true.

"I want to help." Iggy sounded quite upbeat.

"Should we try now, while there is a bit of light left?" Eugene asked.

I was game. I picked up Iggy and stood.

"Where's Hugo?" I asked.

CHAPTER SIXTEEN

"Who is Hugo?" Clive asked.

Whoops. "Pete's lucky charm." I hoped Clive would leave it at that.

Someone knocked on the door. Again? This place was turning into a circus.

"I'll get it." Jaxson opened it, and from his surprised expression, it wasn't who he'd expected.

"May we come in?" That was Genevieve's voice. Her knocking had to be a first, but I was thrilled she was learning that appearing out of nowhere wasn't always a good thing.

"Sure. Clive, this is Hugo and Genevieve. They helped Pete find the body. Like Glinda said, Hugo is Pete's lucky charm."

"Great!" He stood. "I already called Mary Jo, and

she's expecting us, or at least she's expecting me at the house."

"Does she know about Pete and his abilities?" Jaxson asked.

"I told her, but I don't think she believed me."

I wasn't sure he believed it much either. I hoped Pete was still able to do his thing. Since we couldn't fit Jaxson's parents, me, Jaxson, and our two shifters in one car, we piled into our two cars, while Clive drove his vehicle. Genevieve and Hugo could have teleported, but they didn't know where Sid lived—or maybe they did. Since Mary Jo would be home, we didn't want to shock her to death by them just appearing.

Genevieve and Hugo sat in the back of our truck. I twisted around to face them. "Is this the first time you've ridden in a car?"

"Yes, and I'm excited," she said as she glanced out the window.

Pete was with Maddy and Eugene. We both said we'd follow Clive to Mary Jo Harper's house, a trip that took less than ten minutes. The two Harrison family vehicles parked on the street while Clive took up the driveway spot.

Mary Jo opened the front door and stepped out. Her hair was a mess, and she hadn't put on any makeup. Her pain was quite apparent.

We went up the front pathway. Clive reminded her

of who we were and then introduced Hugo and Genevieve as friends of Jaxson's.

She wrung her hands together. "I don't know how anyone can find something that my husband buried forty years ago, but you are welcome to try."

"Should we call the sheriff?" I didn't want this to be an illegal search. Jane Waters was already aware of Pete's talents.

"I called her on the way over here," Clive said.

"Good. How did she react?" I asked.

"The same as always—stoic. But she didn't balk when I said we were going to use Pete here to find the weapon."

She probably didn't think a parrot could get lucky twice. "The big question is whether he can still see under the ground. The spell I did wasn't meant to last forever."

Pete must have heard me, because he flew out of Maddy's hands and landed on the ground in front of me. "I'll have you know that I had some talent without the spell. You and Ruby merely enhanced it."

"I know. Should we get started then?"

Pete didn't answer, clearly miffed at me doubting him. He took off and flew over the house, presumably to begin his search.

"I need to be there," Iggy said.

"You and Hugo both should go. He needs his good luck charms."

"You got that right."

Mary Jo placed a hand on my arm. "Thank you. You all can come through the house to reach the back."

Hugo picked up Iggy and followed us in. While I wished I had the time to enjoy their beautiful home, I wanted to see how Pete would go about his search. I stepped over to Iggy. "Did you explain to Pete how to do a grid search?"

"Kind of. Pete's a little arrogant. This new power of his has gone to his head."

I didn't comment that Iggy had reacted the same way after Ruby had given him the ability to travel through solid objects. "Hugo, would you both stay here until we know Pete needs your help."

Hugo nodded.

Pete was flying about three feet above the ground, which I thought was smart. He started along the west side perimeter and moved south. I assumed with each pass, he'd move closer to the center.

A car door slammed shut. "Mrs. Harper?"

That was Jane Waters.

Mary Jo turned around. "I'll tell her we're back here."

A moment later, Mary Jo escorted the sheriff and her two deputies to the backyard. Both men were carrying shovels, which implied Jane must have believed that Pete could find this knife.

I looked over at our special bird. "Iggy, how about if

you and Hugo ask Pete if he can still see into the ground?"

Iggy looked up at me. "Do you think he'd be flying around if he couldn't?"

I thought it possible since there was a lot riding on this for Pete. If he'd lost his ability, he might not want to admit it. "He might see deeper into the ground if he had some special powerful friends nearby."

"Okay." Iggy and Hugo took off.

I must not have been paying attention to where Genevieve was, but a moment later, she came into view from around the side of the house. I waved her over.

"Where did you go?" I whispered.

"I wanted to ask Pete how things were going, but I didn't think you'd like it if I just teleported from there to here, so I moved out of sight first."

Well, I'll be. Another first. She was becoming more aware of the consequences of teleporting everywhere. "Thank you. So, what did he say?"

"He's good, but he's getting tired."

"No sign of a knife?"

"Not yet," she said.

Pete was moving in a pattern, which was good. When I studied the yard, there were several trees. One in particular looked quite old. "I have an idea." I motioned Jaxson to join me.

"What's up?"

"I want to check out that tree near the far side of the property."

Once we reached it, I waved to Pete who, a moment later, landed at my feet.

"Phew. This is harder than finding a body. Bodies are big. Knives are small."

"That's true, but remember Sid supposedly wrapped it in a shirt, though I can't imagine the shirt would be much more than shredded strips of cloth by now. Anyway, he said he planted it near a tree. This one looks old. How about checking it out?"

"Smart," Pete said. Instead of taking off and hovering above the ground, he hopped and flapped his way around the tree. Oh, boy, at this rate, the light would fade before he'd covered a hundred square feet.

"Would you like some water?" I asked.

"That would be great."

Happy to have something to do, I returned to Mary Jo. "Pete's thirsty."

"He told you that?"

"I thought Clive told you that Pete was special."

She nodded. "He did. I'll get a bowl."

"Thanks."

While Mary Jo went inside to fetch Pete a drink, his search circle widened. Then he slowed. And then he stopped. It looked as if Pete might have found something, or else his X-ray vision was gone.

Mary Jo came out with the bowl of water. "Why did Pete stop searching?"

"I think Pete found something. If you want, you can take the water to Pete. I'm sure he'd appreciate it."

Just as Mary Jo started toward the tree, Pete flew upward and came toward us. When he reached Mary Jo, he landed. She set the bowl on the ground. He told her thank you, but she couldn't hear him.

Once he'd drank his fill, I went over to him and knelt in front of him. "What did you see?"

"I'm hoping it's a knife. It's long and thin and solid."

"That sounds like it might be it." Or it could just be a stick.

Jaxson turned around and waved for the deputies and the sheriff to join him and Hugo. I had no doubt that Pete found something that was not dirt, but was it the knife in question? I was also very curious to see how deep a hole a teenage boy would dig to hide such a weapon. I still couldn't believe he wouldn't have just tossed it in the trash. If this turned out to be the knife in question, then it was a good thing Sid didn't react like I would have.

"Gotta go and show the deputies where to dig." Pete took off.

I followed him. When I arrived at the tree, Jaxson was talking with Pete. Iggy popped up from behind the tree and joined the conversation.

Wanting to stay out of the way, I sat on the ground

and watched as the deputies dug where Pete had indicated the knife might be. They only dug a little dirt at a time. I guess they didn't want to harm any evidence, but it wasn't as if this was some archeological dig.

Genevieve came over and sat down next to me. "This is exciting."

"It will be if there is a knife down there." I don't know why I was being so pessimistic.

"You know Sid never said that Joey Franklin cut Aurora's neck. How will you know it is his knife?"

"The crime happened forty years ago, and apparently Joey was no stranger to the police. They should have his fingerprints on file. Let's hope Sid didn't smudge them too much when he grabbed the knife."

"Don't you think the earth would have eaten away the evidence by now?" she asked.

I turned toward her. "Have you been doing a bit of studying in your spare time?" If there had been better light, I might have seen a slight blush.

"Maybe. There is so much information that Hugo and I missed out on when we were statues on top of that church. A lot has gone on in the last twenty years. Do you know how hard it is to learn how to use a computer at my age?"

"You know your way around a computer?" This I wanted to see.

"I can turn it on and open a few of those picture things on the computer."

I forced myself to keep a straight face. "Do you mean the icons that show you the image of the application?"

"Yes."

"That's great. Keep up the good work. Don't forget Jaxson is really good on the computer." As a math major, I was no slouch either, but I wasn't sure I was up for teaching Genevieve. It was possible she had talents we didn't know about. She seemed to be a quick study about many, but not all, things.

A shout sounded where the men were digging. We both jumped up, and Pete flapped his wings excitedly. One of the deputies held up something. "Well, I'll be."

The officers gathered their shovels and returned to the house. Genevieve and I waited for Jaxson, Hugo, and Iggy. "I can't believe that Pete did it again," I said.

"I had to send him my mojo," Iggy said. He looked over at Hugo. "Or maybe the big man helped."

"Whoever did, I'm sure Pete appreciated it."

When we met up with the others, Mary Jo was almost trembling. "Is that it?"

The sheriff was wearing gloves when she took the knife. "It certainly could be the weapon that Joey Franklin used. We'll have to test it to see if we can lift Franklin's prints."

Mary Jo looked ready to cry. "So you'll let Sid go free?"

"If the knife turns out to belong to Joey, then yes. Any court would say it was a justified killing."

"Thank you, thank you." She looked around. "Where is that bird? I want to thank him."

He landed on Eugene's shoulder. She thanked him and Pete nodded.

"Pete was happy to help," Eugene said.

As soon as the sheriff's department left, we headed out too. Eugene and Maddy offered to stay behind to make sure Mary Jo was okay, but Clive said he'd remain behind.

Clive then thanked us for our help. "I still can't believe you have a magic bird, Eugene."

"I can hardly believe it myself."

We all piled into our cars and returned to Jaxson's parents' house.

"One down, one to go," Jaxson said. "We still need to figure out who killed Armand."

"I'd like to revisit our white board, but let's wait until tomorrow. Today has drained my energy."

Jaxson smiled. "Amen."

CHAPTER SEVENTEEN

No surprise, I tossed and turned all night. Somehow learning that Clive and Sid had been involved in Joey Franklin's death made those two seem more suspect in Armand's murder. Unfortunately, I had no proof, even though both men were at the party. It would have been easy to casually walk up to Armand, stick him in the shoulder with the poison, and walk away.

However, anyone else could have killed Armand. Unlike Sid, who kept the attacker's weapon, I'm sure the syringe was long gone.

No matter how many ways I looked at the situation, I came up empty as to who killed Armand. I really hoped Jaxson or his folks had figured something out.

By morning, after not really sleeping, I climbed out of bed, dressed, and went into the kitchen. Maddy was making breakfast, which was no surprise, and both Jaxson and Eugene were at the counter, drinking coffee.

"Good morning," I said.

"You're up early."

"I couldn't sleep."

"I hear you." Jaxson poured me a cup and motioned I sit down. "Tell me that your restlessness was due to the fact that you have figured out who killed Armand."

"I wish. You?"

Jaxson shook his head. "Unfortunately, no. If we knew what evidence Jane had, we might be able to figure it out."

"True."

Genevieve and Hugo came in. "There you all are," she said.

I wondered if they'd been out and about this morning. "Learn anything?"

"A lot, but nothing we can use—at least that is what Steve would say."

I chuckled at how Genevieve was taking this evidence collection stuff to heart. Steve had taught her well. "That's okay. Knowledge is power," I said.

"I don't know what that means, but this morning, I followed the sheriff, while Hugo decided to revisit Lydia, since she was the closest to the deceased."

"Anything interesting come up?"

"The sheriff tested the knife. After they kind of cleaned off some of the dirt, they used this black powder stuff and poured it on the metal. I don't know why. It made the knife dirtier."

"That was fingerprint power."

"Good to know. Anyway, they then used some tape. She said it lifted something."

"The print. Then what?" I asked.

"The deputy used a computer to compare it to Joey Franklin's print."

She should write a book. She could draw out a story better than anyone. "And?"

Genevieve grinned. "It was a match!"

"That's great!" Eugene said. "That means Sid is innocent."

"Yeah, of that murder."

Jaxson leaned forward. "What do you mean? Did Jane find evidence that Sid killed Armand?"

Genevieve looked over at Hugo. "She thinks she did. A call came into the station. I don't know what was said, but she and her deputies took off and went back to Sid's house."

"Did they let Sid go?" Eugene asked.

"No. They had just found out about the knife when Jane received the call."

"Can we skip forward a few steps? Why did she go to Sid's house?" I asked.

Genevieve planted a hand on her hip. "I'm getting to that. Impatient much?"

She was right. "I'm sorry. Continue."

"We followed them. On the side of Sid's house is a shed. And inside the shed was a small container of the pesticide that killed Armand. They did that black dusting stuff again, but there was nothing—no prints."

That sounded suspicious to me.

"Sid works for a pesticide company. He might have brought some home," Eugene said.

"That's what I thought, but it wasn't as if I could say anything. Jane mentioned it wasn't the kind of stuff you could buy at a store. This was a con...I can't remember the name." Genevieve looked over at Hugo. "Right. It was a concentrated solution."

"I'm sure Jane will figure out what all of this means," Eugene said. "I don't believe Sid would kill again."

"Dad, remember that at the time of the party, we hadn't found the body. Maybe Sid thought that the town would invoke the eminent domain rule and buy back that land. He might have been desperate. I know that Jack Hargrove didn't want to sell, but he wouldn't have had a choice if the city wanted the land for the good of the city."

"True."

Genevieve disappeared, but moments later, she returned right behind Pete who was flying into the kitchen.

"You're starting without me?" Pete asked. "Genevieve just filled me in. I found the knife, and now it won't help Sid?"

"I wish I knew. Genevieve, that was great sleuthing. You didn't say what Hugo found out?"

"This is where it gets really interesting. You would think that finding the poison in Sid's shed would be enough to arrest him, right? Or rather, arrest him again."

Was she planning on becoming a lawyer now? "Maybe."

"Hugo thinks that Bea Jones killed Armand."

Eugene chuckled. "Bea? You think she killed Armand? Why? They were an item, or so I've heard."

Maddy came over to the counter. "Breakfast is ready. Let's eat in the dining room. I think this discussion may take a while."

We all carried out the food and sat down. I couldn't wait to hear what Hugo found out, not that it would be admissible in a court of law, but knowing the truth would help us focus better. "Tell us what Hugo learned."

"Lydia was talking with her sister about what she found in their safe. Apparently, only Armand used it, but Lydia located the combination in his desk drawer. Since he was dead, she thought, why not check it out?"

I could tell Genevieve was waiting for me to ask what was in there. She liked to play this cat and mouse game. "What was in the safe?"

"Evidence about that night at the fairgrounds." She wiggled her eyebrows.

"What kind of evidence?" Jaxson asked.

"It was his diary. Armand had been seeing Bea, aka Trixie, on the side. He wrote how excited he was at first to be with her, but then he started to think that she was only using him."

That was an odd thing for a man to say. "Using him how?" I asked.

"She started asking him why he wanted to put in the strip mall. Bea tried to tell him it was a bad idea." Genevieve looked over at Hugo and then nodded. "He didn't read the diary. This was what Lydia told her sister over the phone."

"Anything else? So far, this doesn't show that Bea killed Armand, unless he told her there was nothing she could do to change his mind."

"Just wait. I'm not finished. Bea, in a state of weakness, told him how she just found out that her sister, Aurora, was really her mother, and that Sid Harper was her father. Bea also told him about the night her mother was attacked and how Sid and Clive helped bury the body. She begged Armand not to go ahead with the city's plan to take over the fairgrounds."

"Whoa. Sid is Bea's dad? Does he know?" Eugene asked.

"Not when it happened. I don't know if he knows now, either."

"If he doesn't know, I wouldn't want to be around when she tells him," I said. "But go on."

"Lydia said she didn't read the whole diary since it

made her sick to her stomach. However, Lydia did find a check book that had various deposits at regular intervals for regular amounts. One was for a thousand a month, another for five hundred a month, and a third for seven hundred and fifty dollars a month."

I whistled. "Are we thinking blackmail here?"

Eugene leaned back in his chair. "Armand was a cool character, but blackmail? I mean, it's possible, but I never would have guessed it."

"Who was the money from?" Maddy asked.

Hugo shrugged.

"There are only three people who had a lot to lose if the information about Joey Franklin's death got out: Sid, Clive, and Bea," Eugene said. "While Aurora might not have done any digging, she watched them bury a body. She might be culpable now, too."

"They were all juveniles," Jaxson said. "The laws might be different than for an adult. They can't exactly put these three in juvenile detention."

"No, I suppose not," his dad said.

I could fill in the blanks. "And Sid didn't want the fact that he killed a man and then asked Clive to help him bury a man to get out either. I might pay the blackmail money too."

"Dad, do you think Clive would be willing to admit he was being blackmailed? He already admitted to burying a dead body. Maybe we could ask him."

"Good. I'll ask Clive and Sharon to come over for

lunch. I refuse to believe that Clive killed Armand. No offense to him, but Clive was a follower, not a leader."

There were some holes in that theory. "How do we know Sharon wasn't behind Armand's murder? She might have gotten a hold of the poison and told Clive to take care of Armand."

Maddy shook her head. "It's possible, but Clive's crime isn't a big one. At least nothing that would warrant a murder to cover it up. And I'm not sure that the statue of limitations hasn't run out. No, if anyone, it would have been Mary Jo who would have asked Sid to deal with his past in a more permanent way. She might have been tired of trying to convince the Council to keep the fairgrounds when any normal person could see it wasn't worth saving."

I'd give all three of them a ten rating, but I really didn't know them as well as Maddy and Eugene did. "I say ask Clive and Sharon over. Sid's still in jail, right?"

"Yes," Genevieve answered even though I had directed my question to Eugene.

"I'll give them a call," Jaxson's dad said. "Since Pete was the one to find the knife, and we know a lot of the story, Clive might be willing to share in order to save his good friend."

Eugene pulled out his cell and called him. After a short conversation, he disconnected. "It took some convincing, but Clive agreed to stop over. He and

Sharon will be here in an hour. Let's finish eating and clean up so we can eat again!"

"If they're coming for lunch, I should run to the diner and pick up some sandwiches," Jaxson offered.

"Thank you," Maddy said.

After we discussed what we would and wouldn't reveal about Armand's diary, we finished our breakfast and then cleaned up. Shortly after Jaxson returned from the store with the sandwiches, Clive and his wife showed up.

Sad to say, they both looked a lot worse than at the Christmas party. And here, I didn't think I'd slept well.

Maddy had made a pitcher of lemonade, which seemed like an odd choice of beverage for the winter, but I could tell by the way she was rushing around, that her nerves had gotten the best of her.

"Did you hear the sheriff thinks Sid killed Armand?" Clive certainly didn't believe in beating around the bush.

"I did," Eugene said. "They found the chemical that killed Armand in his shed."

"I know, but what killer would leave a vial of it around? If Sid was smart enough to wipe his fingerprints, he'd be smart enough to throw the evidence away," Clive said.

I had to say that made sense. "If you're implying that the killer planted the vial in there, who would that be?"

"I wish I knew." Clive turned to Eugene. "I don't know why I'm telling you all this. I realize my wife and you work together, but I get the sense that you believe that Sid is innocent."

"I do," Eugene said.

"Then I need to throw another name in the ring. It's possible that Bea Jones killed Armand."

We all did an excellent job of keeping a straight face. "Why is that?" I asked.

"Armand was blackmailing Bea, Sid, and me. Yes, yes, I know that implies that his murderer might be any one of us, but I know I didn't kill Armand, and Sid is still too torn up about killing Joey Franklin to harm anyone else. That only leaves Beatrix."

"Being blackmailed by itself doesn't mean she's guilty," I said.

"I'll give you that. The only other person with a motive would be Lydia. Who wants to be with a cheater and a blackmailer?"

Clive should have been in our discussion on our suspect list. "Or Daniel Lee. He might have wanted to eliminate the man who his wife was cheating with," I tossed out.

Clive shook his head. "To be honest? I think Daniel Lee was happy she was interested in another man. He was looking for a reason to divorce Beatrix."

Hugo and Genevieve hadn't learned that fact. "Do you have any proof that Bea is guilty?"

"I think so."

"Clive, you need to tell the sheriff," Eugene said.

"I already did." He looked around, clearly waiting for someone to ask what it was.

"What is that evidence?" Maddy asked.

"When I was visiting Sid, he said two days before the Christmas party, Bea came to his office."

That seemed odd. "Why?"

"That's what Sid wanted to know. They weren't exactly close, other than they were both married to people on the City Council."

"Did she want to discuss the fairgrounds issue?" I asked. Or tell him he was her father?

"No. That would almost make sense. She said that since Mary Jo's birthday was the week of New Years, Bea wanted to throw a party for her. Sid was surprised, but he wasn't going to turn her down. Once she left, Sid didn't think anything more about it."

So far, that wasn't pointing a finger at Bea. "How does that make her a murderer?"

CHAPTER EIGHTEEN

"About an hour after Bea left, Sid walked out of his office and found his badge on the floor in front of his office door. And before you say he probably dropped it, he couldn't have. He hadn't left his office, and he needs the badge to get into his office."

"Are you saying Bea took it?"

Iggy had been under my chair the whole time. He poked his head out. "Do I need to spell it out for you?"

Thankfully, neither Clive nor Sharon could hear him. I looked down and nodded.

"She went to the chemical factory to steal the poison. Then she planted it in Sid's shed. Sheesh."

Iggy might be right.

"I believe so, but don't take my word for it," Clive said. "The sheriff is looking through the footage of the office surveillance cameras right now."

"Bea didn't think about that when she went in there? Assuming she took the chemical?" I asked

Jaxson place a hand on my arm. "Trust me when I say that not all criminals make the best choices."

"I guess not."

"Do you have any idea when we'll hear back from the sheriff?" Maddy asked.

"No, but I'm sure she's working as fast as she can."

"Not to be a spoilsport here, but even if the cameras show she took the poison, how can we prove she used a syringe to kill Armand?" I asked.

"She is a nurse, which means she has easy access to syringes." Clive held up a hand. "I know that makes it circumstantial."

"But she has a good motive," Eugene said.

"You should ask Lydia for Armand's diary," Genevieve said.

Genevieve and Hugo had joined us for this discussion since they'd both been at Sid's house when Pete found the knife, but I wanted to sink into the sofa. We'd discussed not telling Clive and Sharon about that at breakfast.

"What diary?"

I was curious how Genevieve would talk her way out of this one. "I think that neighbor guy mentioned it."

Good catch.

"Wilson?" Eugene asked.

"Yes."

I don't think either of our gargoyle shifters were here when Wilson came over, but Clive wouldn't know that.

"Maybe," I said, hoping to save us some embarrassing discussion. "I bet Lydia will turn it in if she doesn't want the sheriff to point a finger at her."

"I hope she will," Clive said. He looked over at his wife. "Thanks for the offer of lunch, but I think we might have a chat with Armand's widow about what was in the diary."

I liked this man. "Good luck."

When he and his wife left, I guzzled down a glass of lemonade. Iggy hopped onto the table, and Pete, who's cage door had been left open, joined us.

"That was good information," Iggy said.

"It was, but we'll have to wait and see what the sheriff discovers," I said.

"Bea has always been a wild card," Eugene said. "I think that was what attracted Daniel Lee to her, but ultimately it was what drew them apart. Armand was a bigger player, and Bea liked that."

"Eugene, it seems to me that Bea was just trying to protect her mother. She didn't want to the world to find out about Aurora's attack and subsequent aid in burying the body," Maddy said. "That's assuming Aurora told her everything."

"Are you defending her?" he asked.

"No, but I can understand why she did it, assuming

she's guilty. No one saw her stab Armand, did they?"

We all shook our heads. Iggy hadn't been in the dining room until after Armand's death, and Pete had been in his cage. Only Eugene could have seen anything.

"If the sheriff reads Armand's diary about Aurora, learns about his blackmail scheme, and has footage of her stealing the chemical, will that be enough to convict her?" I asked.

Eugene shrugged. "I hope so."

Genevieve looked over at Hugo and then back at us. "What if we scare the truth out of Bea—get her to confess? That will speed things up. And I'm not talking about Hugo doing his mind stuff on her," she said.

"Then how?" We still didn't completely understand what Genevieve and Hugo were capable of.

"Okay. Here's the thing. Hugo happened to overhear her mother, Aurora, telling Bea that she had to stop with her obsessive behavior," Genevieve said.

"What?! When was this?" I asked.

"This morning sometime. I guess I forgot to mention it."

What else was new? "Is Aurora in town?"

"Yes."

Sheesh. "What kind of obsessive behavior are we talking about?"

"Aurora wanted Bea to stop trying to protect her. That comment was made after Bea said that she'd taken care of the problem, which got me thinking that maybe Aurora could convince Bea to tell the truth."

My mind could barely keep up. "How?"

"Aurora already told the police about her involvement in Joey Franklin's death. She also told Bea she had to stop using Aurora's past as an excuse to do whatever Bea wanted."

I wasn't sure I followed. "Is Bea a sociopath?"

"I don't know what that means, but I don't think she regrets killing Armand."

"You know this how?" I asked.

"She told that to her sister."

I made the universal symbol for a *time out* with my hands. "Why didn't you tell us?"

She smiled. "Wasn't it more fun to learn what happened on your own?"

"No." I hoped this suppression of evidence wouldn't be a habit. "Tell me again how you are going to get Bea to confess."

"Leave that to Hugo and me."

"No!"

Too late. They were gone. I turned to Jaxson. "Maybe it was a mistake to ask Genevieve and Hugo to help."

Iggy nudged my hand. "Don't ever say that."

"I'm sorry. Hugo is wonderful, but he can't go off and do whatever he wants—or whatever Genevieve wants him to do."

"He never hurts anyone unless that person deserves it."

That might be true. "If you say so."

"Since Jaxson brought lunch, let's not waste it" Maddy said.

"We'll have a bite, but if we don't hear anything by tomorrow, we'll head back home. We've been gone long enough," Jaxson said.

"I understand."

It was really nice to visit with Jaxson's parents again.

We were almost finished eating lunch when the doorbell rang. I doubted that would be Genevieve and Hugo. They would have teleported in and then appeared since it was safe to do so.

Jaxson pushed back his chair. "I'll get it."

When he returned to the dining room, I was really surprised to see Sheriff Jane Waters.

"Sorry to interrupt your lunch, but since you helped prove that Sid was justified in killing Joey Franklin, I wanted to give you an update on Armand Linfield's murder."

That was a surprise. I didn't think she shared anything.

"Who killed him?" Eugene asked.

"May I?" Jane nodded to one of the empty seats.

"Of course and help yourself to the food," Maddy said.

"No, but thank you. We arrested Bea Jones for the murder of Armand."

"Bea? What proof do you have?" Eugene asked. If I didn't know better, I would have totally believed that he was shocked at that news.

"It was a combination of things." She told us about the video at Sid's chemical plant showing Bea going into the back and stealing a chemical. "She used Sid's badge. She was in his office on some personal business and swiped it."

"Stealing some poison doesn't necessarily make her a criminal, does it?" I asked.

"No, but Armand left a diary, and in it, he details everything she told him about her mother, who was the woman Joey Franklin attacked."

"I had no idea." I opened my mouth, pretending as if I knew nothing. I did an admirable job of acting.

"Yes. Armand figured out that Bea was with him only because she wanted to persuade him to stop pursuing the building of the strip mall on the fairground property."

"That all seems rather circumstantial to me," I kind of mumbled.

"You're right, Glinda. It is, but we found a neighbor who saw Bea go into Sid's shed. We believe that's when she planted the evidence."

That I didn't know. "What does Bea say to all of this?"

"She denied it at first, but when I actually arrested her for murder, she became unglued. She actually admitted to killing Armand, but that she believed it was justified. Armand was blackmailing her."

"She confessed?" Eugene said.

"Shocked me, too. Guilty people don't just say they are guilty, but as I said, Bea has become unhinged."

There was only one explanation: Hugo. It was wrong for him to have interfered, but if Bea had killed a man, she should pay.

Jane pushed back her chair. "I just stopped by to say thank you for lending us your bird to help out Sid, and to let you know that the case is closed."

"You're welcome," Eugene said. "I appreciate you telling us about Bea. I have to say, I never would have picked her as a killer."

"Me, neither, but love does strange things."

As soon as Jane left, our two gargoyle wonders appeared.

"Jane arrested Bea," I told them.

"We know. We saw Jane do it."

"Did Hugo help with the confession?" I know I shouldn't have asked, but I couldn't help myself.

She looked over at her cohort. "Actually, no. We heard what Jane told you, but she left out one thing."

"What was that?"

"Daniel Lee said he saw his wife talk to Armand

seconds before he collapsed. What Jane said was true. Bea just lost it."

"Maybe the guilt got to her," I said. Now I felt bad for thinking Hugo had been responsible for making Bea talk. "Even though the information you found out didn't directly lead to the arrest, I'm glad we figured it out—or rather Hugo figured it out."

Genevieve smiled. "It was fun. If you don't need us anymore, Hugo and I are going to head back to Witch's Cove."

Iggy crawled jumped to the table. "Take me with you."

"Iggy, you don't want to drive back with me and Jaxson?"

"It's not that. I want to go back and see Ruby."

I didn't expect that. "Why? I thought you only were kind of friends with her."

"We are, but I want to see if maybe between her and Elizabeth, they can do a spell to let me fly."

"Whoa! Fly? I don't think that's possible."

He lifted his chest. "Did you think that Pete could have super X-ray vision?"

He had a point. "Not really."

"Okay, then I'll ask Elizabeth or Andorra to call Levy. With all that witch power, I should be able to do it."

There was no use fighting him once he had a

mission. "If you can fly, what are you going to do, assuming you don't fall out of the sky in mid-flight."

"I know what you're trying to do, but it won't work. I will not be scared. To answer your question, I want to fly so I can be on equal ground with Tippy."

I wanted to at least sound reasonable, even though I was absolutely saying *no, no, no* in my mind. "Fine. Give it a try, but what if Tippy asks his other seagull friends to help him in the standoff?"

"You're just like Jaxson," he said.

"How so?"

"You are always making outrageous statements, and Jaxson has to make you face reality. You call him a spoilsport."

I laughed. "I do."

"So, can I go? Pretty please?"

He rarely ever said please. "Fine, but wait until Jaxson and I are back before you try this stunt."

"It won't be a stunt."

"Fine, but if you can fly, you have to promise not to ask Hugo to bring you back here so you can show off to Pete."

I swear his eyes widened. Aha, so that was what this was about.

"Whatever," he said.

I guess it wouldn't hurt if Iggy had a few more magical talents. "Do me a favor?

Let everyone know that Jaxson and I are on our way back home."

"Sure thing."

One second he was there, and the next all three of them were gone.

"Do you think magic can be used to enable him to fly?" Eugene asked.

"I have no idea. The more I'm in the presence of beings like Genevieve and Hugo, the less I know about magic." I turned to Jaxson. "But I have all the magic I need right here."

His parents both said, "Aww," in unison.

Jaxson pulled me into an embrace and kissed me. No spell could have made life any better than it already was.

THE END

EXCERPT FOR PINK MOON RISING

What's next? Glinda is in the movies! Too bad there's a murder and a rambunctious raccoon. Check out Pink Moon Rising.

Buy on Amazon or read for FREE on Kindle Unlimited

Don't forget to sign up for my Cozy Mystery newsletter *to learn about my discounts and upcoming releases. If you prefer to only receive notices regarding my releases, follow me on BookBub.*

Here is a sneak peak of book 18: Pink Moon Rising

A movie production in Witch's Cove, a talking bad boy raccoon, and a dead leading lady. Just your typical day in paradise.

I am so excited that I am going to be in a movie! So what if it's not much of a speaking part. Just being around celebrities will be awesome. Or at least it was until one of the leading ladies turned up dead.

It's not that my partner and fiancé in The Pink Iguana Sleuths aren't used to dead bodies, but this case also included a raccoon, who happened to be the leading lady's familiar. It wouldn't be so bad if he hadn't recruited Iggy for his nocturnal misadventures.

Since we suspected magic had something to do with the woman's death, the sheriff actually welcomed our interference (his word, not mine). With a large cast, the suspect list was endless. As daunting as that sounds, between the gossip queens in town and several powerful beings, I'm confident we'll find the killer.

If you want to check up on Iggy and this miscreant raccoon, check the alley behind our strip mall, and you might catch a glimpse of them. They would be happy to fill you in on the latest news.

"How did the shoot go today?" I asked my long-time girlfriend, Penny Carsted.

We had waitressed together for three years at my Aunt Fern's restaurant, the Tiki Hut Grill, in Witch's

Cove, Florida. While she was still working there, I had moved on to running The Pink Iguana Sleuths with my fiancé, Jaxson Harrison.

Did I regret changing professions? Not at all, except that waitressing brought in more money—at least in the beginning it did. Being amateur sleuths, Jaxson and I worked for free unless the client wanted to reward us, which was what happened big time a year ago. We actually received enough money to buy the strip mall across the street, which we use as our source of income.

And speaking of that series of stores, we are currently renting out what used to be the music store to the movie company who is using it as a diner—albeit a fake one. Apparently, the director liked the front and side windows of the shop since it showcased our beach town.

"The shoot was good," Penny said. "I had a scene with the doctor today. Let me tell you that I'm so happy I don't have a real broken ankle. Wearing that boot for a few hours is a pain. Literally. I can't imagine wearing a plaster cast."

Penny and I were hired as extras for the Pink Moon Rising Productions movie, *No Love Potion Needed.* In it, I played a waitress at Sampson's diner where the leading lady also worked. Penny's character was a frequent patient for the new-in-town hot doctor, Ivan Maynard. Because of her *injury*, she needed many appointments.

So far, Penny had not complained about having to be in the same room as him.

"How was Dr. Hottie today?" That was her nickname for the leading man, not mine. I only had eyes for Jaxson.

Even though Penny was practically engaged, she had no problem looking. "He bungled a few lines today, and the director came down hard on him. I felt sorry for Dr. Maynard, but he was kind of rude back."

"That's not good."

"No, but he is the one with all the awards. It's his name that will bring in the viewers, and he knows it."

That was an interesting take. "I rarely interact with him. All I know is that his leading lady doesn't think he has any flaws—or rather the character she plays thinks he's amazing."

Gloria Vega, the leading lady, was a waitress at the same diner where I *worked*. She told me that when the new doctor arrived in town, her character set her sights on him. She thought he really liked her until he hired a nurse who was a real witch. Later on in the movie, we would find out that the nurse puts a love spell on him. I'd say more, but we are only given the script a day or two in advance, and Gloria wouldn't say anything else because of her non-disclosure agreement. Whatever.

Penny sipped her wine. We were having a much-needed girls' night out, opting to stay in at my one-bedroom apartment this evening since it was quiet and confidential.

"I wish I could watch more of the movie being made," Penny said. "It really is exciting, but I'm not around much when Dr. Maynard and Gloria have their scenes, which is sad because that's why I agreed to be in the movie in the first place. I wanted to see them act."

"I hear you."

"You know what bugs me the most?" she asked, though I suspected she wasn't interested in my answer.

"What?"

"The director films things out of order so I can't tell what's really going on. Not only that, I have a day job, and I can't just sit around all day and watch."

"Like me?" I grinned. "Thankfully, Jaxson and I don't have any clients at the moment, so I can hang out a bit more than you."

"Do you think you'll ever do something like this again?" Penny asked.

"Maybe, but only if I have more than ten speaking lines. Even though I play a waitress, no one is allowed to eat the food, and that's just wrong, not to mention wasteful. All I ever do is ask if the person wants more coffee or any dessert."

"I bet Dolly will be sad to see the movie end," she said.

Dolly Andrews—one of the best town gossips and

owner of the Spellbound Diner—made the food that the movie set diner pretended to prepare.

The cat door flapped open and in waddled my nine-pound pink iguana—make that my talking pink iguana. Iggy was my familiar who was quite the character. "Where have you been?" I asked.

"With Bandit."

Ah, yes, Bandit. He was a twenty-pound bad boy raccoon who was the nurse's familiar—or rather the woman who played the nurse in the movie. Because Alexa was one of the doctor's two love interests on the set, the director allowed her to have her raccoon with her. I talked to Bandit on occasion, but I pretended as if I didn't understand his response. I'm sure Iggy already told him that I was faking it.

"What were you two up to?" I asked.

"It was so cool." He looked over at Penny. "Oh, hey. Nice to see you."

Wasn't he Mr. Polite when others were around?

"Hey, Iggy."

My familiar went over to my friend, probably for some attention. When he came near us, I held up a hand. "Hold up right there, mister. You kind of stink. What did you get into?"

"Bandit showed me how to open garage cans. Do you know he can open locks, too? His hands are just like humans—well almost."

"You can't do that, can you?" Iggy's fingers were thin and a bit too flexible.

"No. I don't have strong figures like Bandit does."

"Where were you two while he was showing you all of this Tom foolery?"

"Near Ivan Maynard's trailer. There's a trash can next to his place. Bandit doesn't like him, which is why he wanted to see if he could tip over the can."

"Why doesn't he like Ivan Maynard?" I asked.

"Do you have anything I can eat?" Iggy asked, not answering my question. "Bandit eats anything and everything. He's kind of like the seagulls, except that he makes the mess instead of cleaning it up. But Bandit is better in that he can talk, and he doesn't poop on me."

I chuckled. My poor familiar had an ongoing war with the seagulls at the beach. Iggy truly believed that Tippy, one of the many seagulls, had it in for him.

"Sure. I'll fix you some lettuce." I turned to Penny. "Be right back."

While I went into the kitchen, she and Iggy chatted about his new friend. She also asked him about his best friend, Hugo, but Iggy refused to discuss it. I hope those two hadn't had a falling out.

I fixed Iggy a plate and carried it out. "Here you go. Eat and then it's bath time for you."

"Okay."

Iggy loved water, but he said I was often too rough

with the washcloth. I wouldn't have to resort to such measures if he stayed away from filth.

"Are you working tomorrow?" I asked Penny.

"Only at the restaurant, so you won't see me hobbling around the set. Besides, I just had a *check up* with Dr. Maynard, so I'm not sure when I'm supposed to go back. I think my character has a crush on him. Why else would she keep making up excuses to see him?"

"I think your character definitely has a thing for Dr. Maynard." We referred to the actors by their stage names, since it was too complicated to use both their real names and those of the characters they played. Not only that, I only knew one or two actual names. I mentally remembered my schedule for tomorrow. "I am due on set at nine," I grumbled.

Penny winced. "That's really early for you."

Normally, I slept in until ten or later. "Yeah, but the movie won't last forever."

"True." She finished her glass of wine. "Since I have the breakfast shift, I need to be going. Say hi to Jaxson for me."

I smiled. "I will."

After we hugged goodbye, Penny left. Once Iggy finished eating, I lifted him up. "Time to get clean, Mister Stinky."

"I need to tell Bandit that garbage cans are off limits from now on."

I swallowed a smile. "You do that."

The next morning, I'd just placed some delicious smelling food in front of two actors when the director yelled, "Cut."

I hoped I hadn't been the one to mess up. In case I was, I backed up, though what good that would do, I don't know. The fake diner only had two booths that were situated next to the window and five tables that were spread out in the rest of the small area. The counter was along the back of the room, with the former back room serving as the fake kitchen.

Gloria looked over at the rest of the cast and then turned to Shawn Shields, the director/producer. "What's wrong?" she asked. Shawn was about forty-five, kind of pudgy, and had a beard in need of trimming.

"Where is Alexa? She's supposed to be here." The director sounded rather impatient.

I wasn't in charge of anyone, so I relaxed. I'd heard that Alexa, the handsome doctor's nurse—and Bandit's host—was not completely reliable, but this was the first time I'd heard that she'd missed being the center of attention.

Chris Pena, the author of the book-turned-movie, leaned close to the director. I'd say Chris was probably the same age as Shawn, but he was tall, rather thin, and much better looking.

"You. Need. To. Do. Something. About. Her," Chris ground out.

From what I've read, except for a few really big movies, the writer never had a say in what went on during the production. I guess this guy was too big to say no to—that, or he helped finance this rather small budget movie. On the other hand, these two could be dating.

"I will—or rather, I wish I could."

What did that mean? I was surprised the director didn't keep his voice down.

I looked out the window toward the park to see if perhaps Alexa was on her way over to the set. Only the three main characters merited a trailer. The rest of the cast was staying at the Magic Wand Hotel, which was located down the street—just on the other side of our strip mall.

I was happy for the hotel owners that they'd be booked up for a few months, but they probably would have been full this time of year anyway. It was high season, after all.

Wherever Alexa was at the moment, I hoped she showed up soon.

"Chuck, go find her," the director barked out.

"Where do you suggest I look?" his assistant asked.

The director rolled his eyes. "See if she's at the hotel doing makeup—at least she should be there."

"And if she's not?"

Chris Pena placed a hand on the director's arm. "She might be with Ivan somewhere." He raised his eyebrows, but I didn't know what that meant. "They have a big scene coming up. I'll check in both of their trailers."

"Good." The director turned to Chuck. "What are you waiting for? Go." He then faced the rest of us. "Take five everyone, but stay here."

This was the part of the movie process I found the most distasteful—the standing around. Since it was impossible to know how much time a scene required, Alexa might have decided to arrive on her own schedule. Waiting might not be her thing either.

The movie had only been shooting for a couple of weeks, but during that time, I had the sense that Alexa thought she was someone special. Considering she could have her *pet* raccoon with her, she might be right.

The rather sour and fastidious writer rushed across the street to the park. There were four trailers on the near edge of the park. Three for the main actors and one for the director.

Chris went to the one on far left that belonged to Dr. Hottie. He knocked, and a few seconds later, the actor who portrayed the doctor opened up. Being across the street, I couldn't hear anything. Even if I had the ability to cloak myself and teleport, like a few entities I knew could, it would look a tad odd if I just disappeared from the diner.

Apparently, Alexa wasn't there, because Chris then went next door to her trailer. He knocked, but I didn't see her open up. Either the door was unlocked or she told him to enter, because Chris went inside. I walked over to an empty booth and sat down. I imagine it would take her a while to get ready and come out.

Another cast member joined me in the booth. "There should be a penalty every time you miss your call," Lynn Lurch said.

"Wouldn't that be nice?"

Two minutes later, Chris burst into our fake diner, his face flushed. "I can't believe it. Alexa is dead!"

The director jumped up. "What? Did you call 9-1-1?"

"Why? She's dead."

"How do you know?"

"Trust me. She is."

Not trusting anyone to have it together in this tragic moment, I slipped my phone out of the pocket and called the sheriff's office. Pearl Dillsmith, the receptionist and the sheriff's grandmother, answered the call, but this time I didn't start with my usual friendly greeting.

"Pearl, it's Glinda. One of the cast members is dead. Where's Steve?" I refrained from saying she was murdered, but that was what I was thinking—unless she'd taken her own life.

"He's here. Where are you?"

"I'm at the fake diner." We hadn't come up with a better name for it. "Alexa Brown is in her trailer. It's the middle one."

"I'll send Steve right over."

"Thank you."

So much for my movie debut.

Buy on Amazon or read for FREE on Kindle Unlimited

OTHER BOOKS BY VELLA DAY

A WITCH'S COVE MYSTERY (Paranormal Cozy Mystery)

PINK Is The New Black (book 1)
A PINK Potion Gone Wrong (book 2)
The Mystery of the PINK Aura (book 3)
Box Set (books 1-3)
Sleuthing In The PINK (book 4)
Not in The PINK (book 5)
Gone in the PINK of an Eye (book 6)
Box Set (books 4-6)
The PINK Pumpkin Party (book 7)
Mistletoe with a PINK Bow (book 8)
The Magical PINK Pendant (book 9)
The Poisoned PINK Punch (book 10)
PINK Smoke and Mirrors (book 11)
Broomsticks and PINK Gumdrops (book 12)

Knotted Up In PINK Yarn (book 13)
Ghosts and PINK Candles (book 14)
Pilfered PINK Pearls (book 15)
The Case of the Stolen PINK Tombstone (book 16)
The PINK Christmas Cookie Caper (book 17)
Pink Moon Rising (book 18)

SILVER LAKE SERIES (3 OF THEM)

(1). **HIDDEN REALMS OF SILVER LAKE** (Paranormal Romance)

Awakened By Flames (book 1)
Seduced By Flames (book 2)
Kissed By Flames (book 3)
Destiny In Flames (book 4)
Box Set (books 1-4)
Passionate Flames (book 5)
Ignited By Flames (book 6)
Touched By Flames (book 7)
Box Set (books 5-7)
Bound By Flames (book 8)
Fueled By Flames (book 9)
Scorched By Flames (book 10)

(2). **FOUR SISTERS OF FATE: HIDDEN REALMS OF SILVER LAKE** (Paranormal Romance)

Poppy (book 1)
Primrose (book 2)

Acacia (book 3)
Magnolia (book 4)
Box Set (books 1-4)
Jace (book 5)
Tanner (book 6)

(3). **WERES AND WITCHES OF SILVER LAKE** (Paranormal Romance)

A Magical Shift (book 1)
Catching Her Bear (book 2)
Surge of Magic (book 3)
The Bear's Forbidden Wolf (book 4)
Her Reluctant Bear (book 5)
Freeing His Tiger (book 6)
Protecting His Wolf (book 7)
Waking His Bear (book 8)
Melting Her Wolf's Heart (book 9)
Her Wolf's Guarded Heart (book 10)
His Rogue Bear (book 11)
Box Set (books 1-4)
Box Set (books 5-8)
Reawakening Their Bears (book 12)

OTHER PARANORMAL SERIES

PACK WARS (Paranormal Romance)

Training Their Mate (book 1)
Claiming Their Mate (book 2)
Rescuing Their Virgin Mate (book 3)

Box Set (books 1-3)
Loving Their Vixen Mate (book 4)
Fighting For Their Mate (book 5)
Enticing Their Mate (book 6)
Box Set (books 1-4)
Complete Box Set (books 1-6)

HIDDEN HILLS SHIFTERS (Paranormal Romance)
An Unexpected Diversion (book 1)
Bare Instincts (book 2)
Shifting Destinies (book 3)
Embracing Fate (book 4)
Promises Unbroken (book 5)
Bare 'N Dirty (book 6)
Hidden Hills Shifters Complete Box Set (books 1-6)

CONTEMPORARY SERIES
MONTANA PROMISES (Full length contemporary Romance)
Promises of Mercy (book 1)
Foundations For Three (book 2)
Montana Fire (book 3)
Montana Promises Box Set (books 1-3)
Hart To Hart (Book 4)
Burning Seduction (Book 5)
Montana Promises Complete Box Set (books 1-5)

ROCK HARD, MONTANA (contemporary romance novellas)

Montana Desire (book 1)

Awakening Passions (book 2)

PLEDGED TO PROTECT (contemporary romantic suspense)

From Panic To Passion (book 1)

From Danger To Desire (book 2)

From Terror To Temptation (book 3)

Pledged To Protect Box Set (books 1-3)

BURIED SERIES (contemporary romantic suspense)

Buried Alive (book 1)

Buried Secrets (book 2)

Buried Deep (book 3)

The Buried Series Complete Box Set (books 1-3)

A NASH MYSTERY (Contemporary Romance)

Sidearms and Silk(book 1)

Black Ops and Lingerie(book 2)

A Nash Mystery Box Set (books 1-2)

STARTER SETS (Romance)

Contemporary

Paranormal

ABOUT VELLA DAY

Love it HOT and STEAMY? Sign up for my newsletter and receive MONTANA DESIRE for FREE. Click here

OR Are you a fan of quirky PARANORMAL COZY MYSTERIES? Sign up for this newsletter. Click Here

Not only do I love to read, write, and dream, I'm an extrovert. I enjoy being around people and am always trying to understand what makes them tick. Not only must my romance books have a happily ever after, I need characters I can relate to. My men are wonderful, dynamic, smart, strong, and the best lovers in the world (of course).

My Paranormal Cozy Mysteries are where I let my imagination run wild with witches and a talking pink iguana who believes he's a real sleuth.

I believe I am the luckiest woman. I do what I love and I have a wonderful, supportive husband, who happens to be hot!

Fun facts about me

(1) I'm a math nerd who loves spreadsheets. Give me numbers and I'll find a pattern.

(2) I live on a Costa Rica beach!

(3) I also like to exercise. Yes, I know I'm odd.

I love hearing from readers either on FB or via email (hint, hint).

Social Media Sites

Website: www.velladay.com

FB: www.facebook.com/vella.day.90

Twitter: velladay4

Gmail: velladayauthor@gmail.com

Printed in Great Britain
by Amazon